BLAZING VENGEANCE

The Frost Fervor Concordance Book Three

TOM HANSEN

IceBlazer
Entertainment

For all those who feel trapped.

A man dies when he refuses to stand up for that which is right. A man dies when he refuses to stand up for justice. A man dies when he refuses to take a stand for that which is true.

— MARTIN LUTHER KING JR.

Prologue

Imryll Farora crouched behind the stone pillar as she listened carefully to the discreet padding of enemy feet echo off the stone walls. Flashes of light and shadow bounced off the polished stone, mimicking her pounding heart. Her lungs yearned to gulp for much-needed air, but she forced her breathing to slow and gave her air-starved lungs a chance to catch up.

You will not find me.

Movement to her left made her turn, careful to not make any noise lest it give away her position. Shadows played off the walls, adding to the confusion, but she was ready. She knew how to suss out her enemy, no matter what.

She listened for the tell-tale signs of labored breathing from the next pillar over.

Two can play this game.

She knew they were close, she just needed to get them to show their location.

In one swift motion, she threw a projectile of ice to her left, turned to the right, and sprinted.

As soon as she left the safety of her previous pillar, the ground exploded. Shards of stone and ice blasted in every direction from the impact, pelting her side and leaving her skin raw and inflamed. Luckily, none of it punctured her skin.

That was too close.

She needed a new tactic. The enemy would undoubtedly be changing their strategy for the next move.

Standing, she surveyed the battleground before her. Half a dozen pillars stood in the way between her and her goal, the way out of this place.

If she sprinted directly for it, she would get hit.

Taking each pillar one by one would take too long and give away her plan to the enemy. She had barely made it away from the last one and that was probably only because she shot in the opposite direction.

Damn.

Her enemy wouldn't allow her to make the same move twice.

Time for something daring. Sometimes you just had to take a chance and see where it landed you.

Drawing a healthy amount of magic from the flow of the Concordance, she formed a solid ball of ice around her. More and more she pulled in, hardening it and building up the solid sphere of ice that would to protect her from the onslaught she knew was coming.

Finally, nearly exhausting her supply of magic, she stopped. Imryll was encased in a huge ball of ice over a foot thick. She hoped it would be enough to handle the onslaught she knew was coming for her.

With the remaining bits of magic she had left to her disposal, she nudged the huge ice ball. It rolled with surprisingly little effort, given how perfect a sphere it was.

One.

She steadied her magic, and tensed her muscles.

Two.

She took a deep breath, pushing out all the anxiety and stress in order to ensure she was here, in this moment, focused on this singular task.

Three.

She released her magic.

In a burst of frost, her ice ball shot forward, bounced off of one pillar, and crashed into another one.

Above her, the pillar cracked, and debris rained down on her ice ball.

Again!

She shot herself forward once more.

Crack!

A huge ice spike crashed into her ball, splintering large chunks off her protective barrier. None of it broke through though, as she had planned.

This was it, her last chance to escape, and she had used up too much magic to do anything else. She had to aim this one perfectly, but quickly.

Hurry!

She shot herself forward again, into another pillar. The ice surrounding her was so thick she couldn't see clearly. She should have taken a little more care with her construction to remove all the air from the ice so she could see better, but now it was too late. Now, she just needed to move.

She shot forward again.

Crack! Crack! Crack!

Three ice spikes pelted the back of her ball in rapid succession, leaving a large schism in her protective sphere. She was in the middle of the room, completely exposed with nothing else protecting her.

She was nearly out of energy, but this was her one shot. *I have to be close, right?*

She hesitated, realizing that water dripped off her brow. She wiped it off and stared at it dumbly for a half-second.

Am I sweating?

She didn't know if she should be bewildered or terrified. She hadn't sweat like this in so long.

Her heart continued to pound in her chest as another spike crashed into the ball. This one worked its way through the weaker parts of the ball, breaking through and pelting her side with chunks of ice. The sharpened point stopped less than an inch from her stomach. She broke it off with her hand to allow her to breathe again.

Too close, now go!

She threw herself forward once more, aiming high at the wall to try to deflect off it and land in the middle. If this worked, she would only have to throw herself one final time to escape this fight.

Her sphere hit the wall, but instead of the solid thunk she expected from the thick ice, what she heard was a dull thud. A third of her sphere split off where she hit the wall, crumpling into chunks and removing most of the momentum from her protective sphere.

Imryll bounced, but not enough, landing directly behind the final pillar before she could escape.

She was so close, but would never make it in her damaged ice sphere. A few feet in either direction and she would have had a straight shot to the exit, but here, directly behind the pillar, she was too exposed.

For a second, she thought about making a run for it on foot, but she knew she wouldn't last. She'd poured too much energy into her sphere, and it had failed her.

Imryll let out a sigh. Sometimes it was better to just give yourself over to the mercy of the enemy.

She stuck her hands out of the broken sphere in defeat. "I give up! I give up!"

The hum of magic snapped all around her, that sharp crackle and biting cold she knew so well. A dozen thin ice spears hovered in the air, ready to strike.

Giving herself up was the only correct move here, she knew that now. It was daring, for sure, but the timid didn't change the world.

She poked her head out of her broken ice ball. "I'm coming out now. I'm done fighting."

Meki's bright red hair was the first thing she saw. The little girl panted from exertion, but Imryll knew Meki barely touched her reserves of magic to do this amount of destruction.

"You bested me, little one." She glanced around their arena. Four pillars lay crumbled on the marble floor and six more had huge cracks in them. She would have to have Khatar get those fixed by her stone mages before tomorrow.

Meki smiled and took a small bow. "I told you I would get better." At once, all her ice spikes dropped to the floor, shattering into a thousand pieces.

Imryll let down her hands and walked up to Meki. The little thing barely learned she even had magic a few weeks before, and was already the most powerful frost mage Imryll'd seen in all her years. It was simply incredible watching Meki learn to harness her powers in such a short amount of time. Kids learned so fast, and took to new ideas and methods better than adults.

"That is the third time I've beaten you!" Meki stated, her little fists on her hips.

Imryll counted out on her hands. "I think it's twice."

"Twice? No way! There was the time I hit you with the pillar, and the other time where I reflected back your spear and got your leg, then this time."

Imryll chuckled, squatting down and grabbing the girl for a hug. "You got one of those wrong, my dear."

Meki scrunched up her face. "What do you mean?"

Imryll frowned. "You didn't win this time."

Using up the last of her magic reserves, Imryll unleashed a blast of frost, blowing Meki back toward the center of the arena, and propelling the Frost Queen directly at the door. Imryll's head hit the stone floor with a *crack*, and pain shot through her skull, but she slid across the line and stopped when she touched the door.

"Hey!" Meki shouted from the center of the arena. "That wasn't fair!"

"War isn't fair, my child." Imryll winced at the pain in her head as she stood. "That is the one lesson you must understand above all else. We are at war, and the enemy will never rest until you are dead. You can always change a situation for yourself, lull the enemy into a false sense of security, or divert their attention to something while you steal their power. As long as you are alive, you can still fight."

Imryll put her hands on her hips. "As long as you win, it was worth the gamble. If you die, you won't be around to worry about the mistakes you might have made."

Chapter One

Ynya Oblique ground her teeth as Synol said her goodbyes for the ninth time.

"You shouldn't do that. You can't regenerate your teeth like I can." Finny said in her matter-of-fact manner.

Ynya rolled her eyes. "I'm well aware that I shouldn't do it, I just don't care. I want Synol to hurry up."

"Then why don't you just tell her that?"

Ynya looked over at her sister. In the four weeks they'd been traveling together, Ynya still had a hard time knowing if Finny was making a joke or not.

Finny had always been a very literal girl, and it was cute when she was younger. But whatever torture they did to her as part of the Enlightenments back at Reyoarfjell had changed her into something Ynya wasn't quite sure how to handle.

Finny's mind wasn't the same one that had entered that facility weeks ago. Sometimes she was caring and warm, other times she was cold and literal to a fault. Others, she was brimming with rage and pain and refused to talk to anyone.

The last one was the one Ynya worried about most. She

knew the rage, she had spent her whole life bathed in its fiery heat, but she had changed in the last few months. She was at war, and war changed you. Sometimes you had to make tough choices in order to squeak by. Loss and anguish followed her everywhere she went now. No matter what choice she made, someone ended up getting hurt, and Ynya wasn't sure she could live with the consequences of her decisions.

When she had first found her parents slaughtered, she had made a choice of who of her sisters to rescue first. Ultimately, she had rescued Synol, and Ynya wondered if she shouldn't have just continued her pursuit after the two younger ones instead. Yes, Synol needed saving from her horrible husband, but the cost to Finny's mind and body had been great.

She hoped it hadn't been too much.

Ynya looked at her sister. Despite being four years younger, Finny was now as tall as Synol, but lacking the mature features you normally got with age. Ynya wondered if Finny would continue to grow as she aged. It was something Finny had decided to do when she transformed from the beast on the table back to her human form.

Ynya pursed her lips and nodded at Synol. "It's the polite thing to do, to allow her to say goodbye in the manner she prefers. Besides, these people risked their lives just giving us shelter.

"But she is frustrating you and you should tell her so she stops."

"If I just grabbed her and pulled her away, then she and I would have an argument." Ynya grabbed the bridge of her nose and squeezed. It was an action she'd seen her mother do a thousand times growing up, as she tried to keep her own anger down and not yell at her petulant little fire-headed daughters.

"Any frustration I feel is my own, it's all in my head. Just because she might be doing something that bothers me doesn't mean it's her fault. Does that make sense? I'm the one *choosing* to be irritated. Synol isn't doing it on purpose, and if I drag her into my own problems, then I have just spread my own frustration to others. That's not fair to her."

Ynya paused, realizing she sounded just like her mother. *Ugh!*

In fact she was pretty sure that was an exact Talia Oblique quote.

"The point is, she's not *being* irritating, I'm the one *getting* irritated. It's my problem and not worth a fight with Synol." A little smirk crossed her lips as she pulled a small vial from her belt. "Though that won't stop me from dumping some fire ants into her bedroll tonight."

Finny looked at the vial for a second before a broad smile crossed her lips. She let out a loud guffaw. "Oh that will be so funny watching her crying from all the bites on her legs!"

Ynya put the vial away as Synol turned in their direction. "Well, I can't do it now, because you just gave it away."

Finny stopped laughing. "I'm sorry. I didn't realize how loud I was just now."

Ynya patted her sister's arm. "It's fine, but I think that gave us our exit finally."

Synol joined them a few seconds later. "I'm sorry, I didn't realize I had kept gossiping so long. What was that about bites on legs?"

Ynya glanced at Finny, whose eyes were bright with pleading mischief. Ynya shook her head slightly. "Oh, nothing. So how are they?"

Synol frowned. "They are more worried than they let on. It's dangerous for them to put us up for so long this close to the

Frost Queen's lair. Her family would have serious ramifications if word got out."

"We kept our hair covered the whole time we were here. I don't think anyone noticed."

Synol frowned again. "I'm not sure that is enough. Three women traveling by themselves this close to Fellsstrond Castle is enough to raise a few eyebrows, let alone the fact that there is basically no one in the Skarfanes that isn't wearing a uniform."

Rather than replying, Ynya kept marching.

Finally, Synol stopped them and pulled Ynya into a big bear hug. "Thank you for waiting patiently, I just had such a hard time leaving them knowing that I probably sentenced them to death for their hospitality. I know you wanted to be there by now, but I just–"

Ynya hugged back. "Take the time that you need, Synol. I know how much it means to you. We will get there when we get there. Besides, it's not like hugging the people who gave us a warm bed is the only thing keeping us from getting there."

Ynya, despite her trepidation at how long it was taking to cross the Skarfanes, knew this was going to take time. They had been in enemy territory for weeks now, and their every step had to be planned carefully.

Too much rode on their caution, and balancing that with speed was just one of the many things that kept her up at night.

Who knew what the Frost Queen was doing to her sister at this very moment. After seeing the atrocities they did to the prisoners in Reyoarfjell, Ynya had a terrifying new understanding of human nature.

And she wasn't sure she liked being part of the populace anymore.

How one person could do those things to another was beyond her. Killing, she understood. Sometimes it was needed, sometimes there was no other choice. If one is forced to kill, at least do it humanely, quickly. End their life with the least amount of suffering to protect your own.

But torture, and the dastardly games the Warden did to his victims, that was just suffering for suffering's sake.

No amount of suffering validates the end result. You can't justify violence against someone unless you are saving your life or the life of someone else.

You just can't.

"Ynya?" Synol frowned at her. "You okay?"

Ynya nodded. "Yeah. Sorry, I'm just tired is all."

While that statement was true, it wasn't the only reason she had been in her head so much lately. The reality of why Ynya hadn't been getting after Synol to hurry up and get Meki back was that Ynya was terrified of what she would have to do once she got there.

So far, they had avoided most of the patrols, and only had to take out the occasional soldier who discovered them.

But Synol or Finny had done all those killings.

Ynya had allowed them.

She didn't know if she could kill again. She didn't know if she could justify it in the name of her safety.

Ynya shuddered with the thought. Reyoarfjell had clearly changed her outlook on life.

She had changed more than she thought in the last couple months, and it terrified her to realize it.

She reached into the pocket containing the magic-preventing earrings she had saved from being buried with Reyoarfjell when it was torn down.

Part of her knew they might come in handy.

Chapter Two

"Hold!" Finny put out her hand to stop her sister's hiking. Finny crouched down to the snow, dropping to all fours as she peered out into the miasma of gently falling snow.

It had been two more days of trudging through the cold. Ynya may not have understood everything about her younger sister sometimes, but she had learned to stop when Finny insisted.

Despite all the damage they had done to her mind, Finny's senses had been significantly enhanced.

While Finny hadn't told them specifics of what had gone on in that chamber, the one thing Ynya could never stop thinking about was the way Finny's body looked while strapped to the table.

Watching Finny sniff the air, down on all fours like a dog, brought those memories back with a vengeance.

Ynya couldn't shake the image. Gods Above, she had tried.

At times, even in her human form, Finny seemed almost feral, like now when she sniffed the air.

What was she sniffing? What could she possibly smell in this blinding snow?

Finny retreated, still on all fours.

Ynya couldn't help but notice that Finny's hands had changed. Instead of the milky white skin and delicate fingers of her twelve-year-old sister, Finny's hands had elongated to twice their length, turned black as pitch, and talons replaced her fingers.

Ynya swallowed, trying to push down the terror that built at the bottom of her skull.

She is still Finny, your younger sister, no matter what she looks like.

Only she wasn't. Finny had changed. They all had, Finny with the most physical changes. Ynya slowly raised her hand to feel the scabbed-over part of her ear where she had forcibly removed the earring to get her magic back.

"What is it?" Synol finally asked in a whisper, her voice barely audible over the howl of the wind.

"An army," Finny said, not taking her gaze off the snow in the distance.

"Army?" Ynya asked, squatting down. She squinted through the haze. "I don't see anything."

Finny tapped her nose, her hands having already regained their human skin and pallor. "Smell. There are a lot of them in the valley ahead of us."

The two older sisters shard a glance.

"How many?"

Finny turned and took a couple more careful steps through the snow toward the edge of the cliff on which they stood. She sniffed the air again, then came back. "Many hundreds, maybe a thousand or more."

"We must be close," Synol said.

Ynya shook her head, trying to decipher this new revelation. "We knew we were, but why is an army outside of Fellsstrond Castle?"

Frustration flashed across Synol's face as she turned to Ynya. "Why wouldn't it be? She's the Frost Queen of the North, wouldn't you want an army to protect you?"

Ynya pursed her lips. "I didn't mean it like that. Why is the army right outside her doorstep? Keeping a small contingent of guards I get, but a thousand, all just outside? That's not just protection, that's amassing for something."

Synol huffed. "We'll take them all down if we have to."

Finny smiled. "Of course we will. Right, Ynya?"

Ynya nodded, but she hadn't really paid attention to the words her sisters said. She was entranced by the pointed teeth in Finny's mouth.

***

Finny disappeared soon after, running off into the freezing cold once the sun had gone down. Ynya used her heat to carve out a safe spot for them to sleep while Synol prepared something to eat.

Ynya couldn't keep it in any longer. "Do you not worry about her?"

Synol paused and looked over. "Finny?"

Ynya nodded. "What did they do to her in that room?"

Synol pursed her lips. "If she's not going to talk about it, then I'm not going to bother her to give me details about something I barely want to know."

"But she's our sister, don't you think we should at least bring it up to see if there is anything we can do to help her?"

Synol looked at Ynya with a curious expression. "You sound more and more like Mother every day, you know that?"

Ynya frowned. "I always thought that was you, you look so much like her, you know. It's almost—"

"Almost scary?"

Ynya huffed. "Sometimes in the middle of the night I see you sleeping and I can't help but remember Mama frozen in the snow."

A silence permeated the camp after Ynya's last confession. She felt bad for comparing Synol to her Mama, but the similarities were too obvious to ignore.

Ynya opened her mouth to apologize when Synol spoke up.

"Have you figured out what her magic is yet?"

Ynya shook her head. The honest truth was that she had been avoiding trying. Ever since Reyoarfjell she questioned her own magic so much that she wondered if she should even attempt to figure out her own mother's magic. What was the point of having access to more magic if people were just going to use it to hurt others?

Ynya focused on the magic in her heart. Her mother's crisp, stoic magic still sat right next to her innate heat after all these weeks. Immovable and unchanging, it strummed along to her heartbeat in perfect time.

Ynya wondered if the magic controlled her heart more than her heart controlled it.

She tried touching it, but recoiled as she made the connection. It was so incredibly powerful that it shocked her every time she did so. It was like touching lightning in a bottle. The thought that her mother had spent her entire life with this powerful and mysterious magic terrified Ynya to her core.

It wasn't the only question Ynya had swirling around in her head, either. Ever since the Warden had shown her the book with her mother's name in it, Ynya couldn't shake the notion that her mother was much, much older than she had seemed.

Ynya looked at Synol again, shocked by just how much her mother looked like her daughter. "Mama looked like you, Synol."

"You said that."

"No, I mean she didn't look like an older version of you, I meant she looked *just* like you, like she was twenty years old."

Synol chuckled. "That's why Papa married her, she looked so young."

But she wasn't.

Ynya wasn't sure how to interpret that realization, either.

Was her mother incredibly blessed by the Gods, or was she just fooling everyone around her all this time?

Synol finished cooking and divided the meal into thirds. She and Ynya and began to eat in silence.

As they did, Ynya couldn't help but test touching her mother's magic again and again. Each time she did, the shock lessened. Knowing it was coming and preparing herself for it helped.

After a half dozen tries, she was still no closer to figuring it out. She put the final bite in her mouth and looked up at Synol, who was barely halfway done with her meal.

"I think I'm going to head to bed early. I have a feeling something big is going to happen tomorrow."

Chapter Three

❦

Finny returned before sunrise, changing from her feral form to her human one just as she entered their camp. She was naked, carrying her old clothes in one hand.

It wasn't the first time Ynya had been awake all night to observe this habit. Too many thoughts and worries swirled in her head all night, keeping her mind from clearing and preventing much-needed rest.

Finny frowned at Ynya for a moment before donning her clothes once again.

They shared too many of these unspoken glances lately, but Ynya could never bring herself to bring it up during the daytime, or follow Finny when she left during the night. Likewise Finny had never brought up the fact that Ynya was frequently awake when she returned to camp.

"Synol, it's time to wake up."

"What's going on?"

Ynya sat up, her eyes not leaving Finny's face, still smeared with blood. Ynya gave her the sign to pay attention, then pointed at her own mouth.

Finny noticed the sign and her eyes widened. She turned and wiped her mouth off with the sleeve of her coat. Cleaned, she pointed out over the ridge.

"There are a little over three-thousand soldiers amassed already, with more coming in by the hour. The camp is laid out in a logical and hierarchal manner, meaning they are very organized. Any new troops arriving are directed to a pre-determined location. The Frost Queen is planning something with her soldiers, that is for sure."

Synol looked over at Ynya. "If all the soldiers are here, then the rest of the country might be safe?"

"We killed over a hundred soldiers, possibly more before going to find Finny, and Hyndalskyr has to be one of the most remote districts in the realm. I'm sure she's leaving solders to keep an eye on the citizens in other districts, but this many coming together means she's gathering all her available resources for something big."

"Taking back the Hyndalskyr district?"

Ynya shook her head. "This large an army would be overkill for something like that. It's all fishermen and small villages. A hundred would be enough if they just coordinated properly."

Synol pounded a fist into her open palm. "Then we just need to summon enough earth, wind, and fire to kill these bastards right where they stand. That should put the fear of the Gods Below into the Queen. Once they are all dead, we can just march into the Castle and take Meki back."

Despite the early morning, Synol's expression seemed like that of a battle hardened soldier. Her eyes gleamed with an intensity Ynya had never seen before.

Ynya was both proud and a little scared of Synol at that

moment. It was amazing how much the two had changed roles since they began their adventure.

Regardless of the gleam in Synol's eye, however, Ynya couldn't shake the fact that something was amiss this morning. The air about them was tinged with smoke, something that should feel normal given a large encampment of soldiers not too far away, but there was something else going on. Ynya just couldn't quite sense what it was.

The rhythm of the world somehow seemed off.

Finny smiled. "I like this idea. If we take them out now, before they have a chance to fully wake up, they will never know what hit them."

"We can't just sneak around to get inside?" Ynya asked.

Finny shook her head. "Fellsstrond Castle is built into the mountain, and there is only one entrance, through the front. I suppose we could backtrack and follow the tops of the Razor-claws and climb down the mountain to enter through a window, but that's our only other option if we want to make it to Meki."

Ynya wanted to argue. Something about this plan just seemed ill-advised, but at the moment, and without the clarity a good night's rest usually brought, she couldn't think of anything else that might go wrong. Even if they killed half of the Frost Queen's army, that was half the soldiers they had to deal with. They could always regroup and take out another half, then again.

Sooner or later, they were going to have to make it through that mass of soldiers to get to the gates, so it was either sneak through, and deal with them on the way out, or rout them now and have an easier time once they rescued Meki.

Either way, they were going to have to do something. She

hoped that their actions wouldn't put Meki's life at risk. Sneaking in seemed to be the most prudent way to keep Meki safe. Ynya worried what the Frost Queen might do if she found out half her army had been destroyed. But the other two wanted to try to frontal assault approach, and Ynya was outvoted.

The three devoured enough food to feed a large horse. They would need significant energy if they were going to make any serious dent in the troops.

Finny led the sisters to the top of another rise overlooking the valley. As the sun rose to the east and cleared out the fog in the valley, Ynya got her first true look at the Frost Queen's lair.

Fellsstrond Castle wasn't much of a castle, per-se. The whole thing had been carved into the sheer cliff-face of a mountain hundreds of years ago before the Queen took over and remodeled to her satisfaction. A gaping opening at the bottom allowed entry, and scattered up the side of the cliff were dozens of cutouts, many with balconies, allowing light and air into the structure.

Inside must be a maze of rooms, staircases, and corridors. It would be a nightmare to navigate once they got in.

Assuming we get in alive.

Spread out before the castle was a large open plain where the three-thousand soldiers camped.

The campsite was huge, half a mile in each direction, if not larger.

Finny wasn't kidding, there were a lot of them here, and they were organized.

All of the army's meticulously laid out tents faced the center, where there was a large circular space devoid of any structures. To the north of the clearing, mirroring the massive mountain cliff to the north, was a large tent where the leader of the army most likely resided. Four slightly smaller, but equally impressive tents ringed the center, possibly lieutenants or captains of smaller divisions.

"We ready?"

Ynya didn't bother nodding. She would follow their lead, and call upon her magic when instructed. "Are you pulling up the flammable gas again?"

Synol squirmed, "I don't think I can make a wall large enough to go around the entire camp. Finny, can you use your wind to collect everyone into the center? Then I will raise up the walls."

Finny nodded, and turned toward the mass of tents. Wind tousled her hair as she pulled magic to her.

"Go!"

Synol knelt, placing open palms to the rock beneath her. All around them, slight tremors in the earth rumbled, a testament to Synol's impressive magic.

Finny stood by her side, hands low to the earth while she swayed with an unseen breeze.

Magic swelled around the two, so much that Ynya took a cautionary step back. It still stunned her how much raw energy each of her sisters controlled, and how easily they manipulated such large areas of their world through their power.

Ynya had never known power that immense. Hers was more personal, focused, but was also severely limited in scope. While they could cast spells far away from themselves, she needed to touch something in order to heat it.

In her chest, Ynya's heart beat soundly against her ribs.

Lub-dub. Lub-dub.

She knew she was excited, but her heart beat was so prominent it distracted her from her sister's casting for long enough that she glanced back to the center of the camp, where two lone figures stood.

A chill ran down Ynya's legs and arms at the sight. Where once there had been an open plain, devoid of anything but unspoiled snow, two shadowy figures now stood.

Ynya felt the surge in magic climax as Synol and Finny finished pulling their energy to them and set to release it in a catastrophic display of prowess.

Ynya concentrated on the center again. Why, with thousands of soldiers, would two lone figures be standing in the center...and why would they be staring up at this one spot on the mountain?

Terror gripped Ynya.

We've been spotted!

Ynya focused on the two lone figures. No other soldiers looked up where the Oblique sisters stood on the rise. No one else stopped their jobs to turn and look, so why had two random soldiers walked out to the middle of a large field to do so?

And why is one of them half the size of the other?

Then it hit her.

Both figures were too thin to be toughened soldiers.

Ynya took a half step back at the realization. She wasn't looking at two random soldiers, she was looking at the Frost Queen and Meki Oblique, standing side by side.

Chapter Four

✿

"Stop!" Ynya yelled. She jumped at Synol, desperately trying to get her sisters to stop casting.

Lub-dub. Lub-dub.

Ynya's heart pounded in her chest again, this time the beat was slower, purposeful.

Ynya grabbed Synol's arms and wrenched them from the ground. She took a step forward, then another.

Lub...dub. Lub......dub.

She did the same to Finny, tripping both sisters and careening them backwards into the snow.

Ynya looked back at the two stationary figures in the distance. Neither had moved.

Neither had even blinked, she imagined.

Around her, all the pent-up surge in magic dissipated just before it crashed forth in a violent display of power. The rumble in the earth subsided, and the electrical charge in the air from Finny's magic ceased, leaving behind a stringent smell on the morning breeze.

Both sisters lay on their backs, bewildered looks on their faces.

Lub-dub. Lub-dub.

Ynya's heart returned to normal, pounding rapidly against her ribs.

What just happened?

She'd managed to stop both of her sisters from killing Meki, that's what had happened.

"What did you do?" Synol spat.

Finny jumped to all-fours, her eyes wide and feral.

"I stopped you from killing Meki."

Synol narrowed her eyes. "Meki isn't down there."

Ynya turned, pointing. "Right there, in the center. She is standing with the Frost–" Ynya's voice failed as she stared at the blank area in the middle of the camp. Seemingly unbeknownst to the imminent destruction, soldiers milled about, readying cooking fires and doing their morning chores. Had none of them even noticed their leader standing among them?

Did I imagine it all?

Ynya's heart sank "But..."

Synol jumped to her feet, a look in her eye that Ynya hadn't seen since they were in the cave with Synol's husband.

Terror gripped Ynya's heart at that look. She had messed up bad. Maybe her overthinking of her use of magic was leading to hallucinations. "Synol, I swear, she was down–"

Crunch!

Something slammed into the ground at Ynya's feet, blocking her view of Synol. It was large, white, and shiny.

It was ice.

Oh no.

Another ice spike slammed into the ground to her side, then again, and again, forming a tight barrier around her body.

Synol screamed and Finny roared. All around the three sisters, ice spikes fell from nowhere in rapid succession, trapping them in human-width ice prisons.

Fiery rage flooded Ynya's chest. She pushed the heat into her hands, grabbing one of the spikes and shearing it in half.

Before her was Meki, standing side-by-side with what had to be the Frost Queen.

The Queen was a lot shorter than Ynya had imagined. She had darker colored skin that was a rarity this far north.

If Ynya had to pick someone to be the Frost Queen, she would have picked someone else. Hell, her own mother with her crazy eyes and wild untamed red hair seemed more likely to be an evil tyrant than this woman before her.

Still, the Frost Queen was impeccably beautiful with smooth, brown skin, large sharp eyes, and a fierce stance that accentuated her slender, taut figure. She was muscular as well as feminine.

She also had oddly pointed ears that Ynya had never seen on a human before. Long white hair cascaded down her back, glimmering like new-fallen snow in the morning light. Her eyebrows were also white, a stark contrast against her skin, but they looked good on her.

Almost too good.

Ynya couldn't help but bathe in the sheer power the Queen held. A frozen edge clung to the air all about them, powerful and razor-sharp, ready to cut anyone who stepped out of line.

"Meki!" Ynya called out. "It's Meki!"

Meki threw out her hands. Another spike slammed into the ground in front of Ynya. "Halt, before you do something you will regret!"

Ynya reeled, bumping against the icy spikes behind her back. *Had...Meki just cast an ice spell?*

"Meki?"

Ynya glanced around. Both of her sisters were also cocooned in their own smaller icy version of what Synol had planned for the camp below.

No one moved, but the fiery rage in Ynya sprang up again at notion that Meki had been the one to cast the icy prison cells and not the Frost Queen.

Meki didn't even have magic! She was too young! She hadn't bloomed yet!

Words from their dying mother echoed through Ynya's memories.

Promise me you will rescue them all, don't leave any behind. Meki will be blooming soon and you need to be there before it happens. Keep them safe.

Ynya had failed yet again. They had taken too long to arrive here, and the Frost Queen had gotten her talons into her sister.

Ynya flared her heat once again and melted the ice around her, vaporizing it so fast that it cracked and sputtered. Dozens of smaller chunks fell to the ground.

"Ynya Oblique." The Frost Queen spoke. Her voice was foreign, with a thick syrupy accent unlike anything Ynya had ever heard before. "It is so nice to meet after all that I have heard about you. I'm quite impressed with how fast you reacted to keep your sisters safe."

The woman's voice was like rubbing your face with silk. No wonder she had become the queen of the north. No man would be able to resist such a sultry voice.

Ynya herself was having a hard time resisting as feelings she hadn't felt very often percolated to the surface.

The Queen stepped forward, side by side with Ynya, focusing on Synol and Finny in their individual icy prisons.

Ynya reeled at the sheer strength of magic flowing off the woman. Like large ice sheets calving off a floating glacier, she exuded so much power that excess rolled off of her body.

No wonder this woman ruled the land. She was the most powerful mage Ynya had ever met.

She was power incarnate, and incredibly alluring to boot.

She was also very close.

All Ynya had to do was reach out, grab the Queen, and pour heat into her head. For a split second, she imagined herself ending it right here, right now. All it would take was a fast motion from her, and the four sisters would be headed home after a warm breakfast.

All this lead-up, all this preparation, and pain, had led up to this singular moment.

But Ynya's mind caught up with her reaction, and she wondered if it would be that easy. *Take one life to save another?*

No, this was the Frost Queen and Ynya was barely an arm's length away. The tyrant of the north! Thousands had been captured, tortured, and killed in her name.

Ynya's magic disappeared in the next heartbeat.

Ynya searched inside herself, for the magic that was supposed to be there. Just like if she had been stabbed by one of the Skarmyord, her magic still hummed, but was so diminished that she couldn't access it. The wells had run dry. She looked down, checking her body for puncture wounds, but she saw none.

Just being beside this woman made my magic stop?

The Queen snapped her fingers, and the remaining icy prisons shattered, falling to the ground in a pile of glittery dust.

Synol glared at the woman, while Finny stared openly, her bright eyes wide with alarm.

The Queen spoke.

"I formally welcome the entire Oblique clan to my home at long last. I'm surprised that you took this long to meet me. I thought I made it very clear to my soldiers that you were allowed safe and swift passage. And yet, for some reason you took your sweet time meandering to meet your sister."

She chuckled to herself in her high-pitched accented voice. "Perhaps you thought you still had to sneak? Maybe you didn't realize that you were all my invited guests?"

She turned, her robe flaring out behind her. "Still, I'm glad that you are finally here, because I have a feast planned for your arrival and we should hurry before the food gets cold."

The Queen turned to face Meki. "Do be a dear and escort your sisters to the dining room. I don't want to keep the chef waiting much longer."

Meki looked up at the woman and nodded with a slight bow. "Of course, Mother."

Chapter Five

M*other?*
  Mother!?!

The group was deathly silent as they walked through the campsite.

Meki was the only one who made any noise, and most of that was her humming a tune while she skipped down the path between the tents.

At least she was allowed to occasionally be a little girl despite living under the thumb of the tyrant of the north.

The Frost Queen stayed behind while the girls followed their sister, but even after retreating a distance from her, Ynya's magic never came back.

"I should tell you that Mother doesn't like it when anyone casts magic around her without her permission. She took your magic from you until you can learn to control it properly. She does it to me sometimes, but you will learn soon enough. She will teach you how to use the magic you didn't even have to do some amazing things!"

Meki continued to skip and hum.

Ynya shared a glance with Synol and Finny.

Together, all four Obliques marched down the central corridor between the tents.

A harsh morning breeze bit into Ynya's skin now that she no longer had her magic to keep her inner temperature high. Despite getting used to the biting cold when she was in Reyoarfjell, she had grown accustomed again to having her inner fire. She liked that fire, it was part of her. It had always been a part of her. She liked being warm.

All around them, the soldiers cleaned their tents, re-organized their bedding, and cooked food. A few gathered on the outskirts, coordinating drills with swords and pikes.

Everyone in the camp seemed highly organized. The angle of their tents, the ropes keeping them from blowing over in the wind, and every bedroll seemed to contain the exact same type and style of blanket. Soldiers cleaned their pots and pans the same. They marched between tents on pre-determined paths, turning at regular intervals. Even the swordplay took on a rhythmic clang from the metal on metal. The whole scene was incredibly surreal.

It felt manufactured. It felt fake. It was almost like the Frost Queen was putting on a show but hadn't quite breathed true-life into her stringless puppets.

While they marched, Meki continued to hum like she was still back in Marsfjord. The skipping was new. She'd been known to skip, of course. What young girl hadn't? But the skip was in time to the same rhythm that seemed to permeate the entire camp.

Clang, hum, clang, hum.

It was like an invisible heartbeat guided the actions of everyone around her.

Ynya found her own heart beating to that same drum, her footsteps falling in line with the rhythm.

She hesitated, waiting a half-second longer to place her foot down, but Synol bumped into her from behind.

"Hey!"

"Sorry." Ynya fell back in line before turning her head and addressing Synol again. "Have you noticed the beat?"

Synol grew silent, but nodded.

Every step increased the tension in the air between the five women. Every crunch of boot against the frozen ground reminded Ynya that she was not safe. She was deep in enemy territory and she was going to be taken to the castle for breakfast?

She couldn't fathom how wrong this all felt. Synol must have felt the same thing because she refused to meet Ynya's gaze.

Finny looked toward the mountain with an expression of fear that Ynya hadn't seen since they were kids.

After glancing at her younger sister three times, and realizing Finny's expression hadn't changed, Ynya veered sideways and took Finny's hand her hers.

Finny hesitated, then returned the squeeze, but her face never changed. Her eyes burned with a feral intensity as she had locked onto some specific point in the castle and refused to move.

No one spoke for a while after that.

Meki led them through the central location where Ynya had seen her and the Frost Queen stand. The large expanse was almost a foot deep of freshly-dusted snow, meaning despite the camp's constant movement of thousands of soldiers, none went through the center.

In the center of the large circle, however, were two fresh sets of boot prints.

What terrified Ynya the most, was the lack of any footprints leading up to or away from those lone prints. Two sets of boot prints, one large one small, marred the center in the large snow-covered circle.

At least I didn't imagine them being here.

Ynya nodded to Synol and gestured to the prints. Ynya stole a glance back at the Queen, who walked behind them with steady, sure feet, yet still seemed elegant as she trudged through foot-deep snow.

Synol nodded, her face sullen. She pursed her lips and furrowed her brow. Synol looked so much like their mother at times, and this was one of them. Ynya remembered her mother trying to figure out how a fishing hook had managed to get caught in her husband's ear and a young Ynya saw that same expression now on Synol's face.

A gust of biting cold snapped her back to the present.

Ynya wondered just how varied the Frost Queen's powers were if she could teleport two people to the center of the camp and away just as fast. The only person she'd known with teleportation powers like this was the woman in black.

Nora.

It was a name Ynya would never forget. It was the name of a woman Ynya hoped to meet again, for many reasons.

As their group of four trudged through the thick layer of snow, Ynya realized just how serene the inner circle was with its undisturbed snow. So much beauty and serenity in the midst of a camp full of murderers and tyrants.

She remembered how the Pit was in the center of Reyoarf-jell, and how, once again, the prisoners of the place were the ones walking through the center while the soldiers and guards went about their jobs on the outside.

A pall fell on her as she realized that yet again, she was without her magic. No matter how hard she tried, her enemy always found a way to remove her fire.

Ynya had changed, though. Growing up she had not only relied on her magic to do almost everything, but she largely defined herself by that one aspect. Even though she was capable of so much else, the part that made her special was what she obsessed about, to the exclusion of other aspects of her life. She hadn't exactly made it easy for her sisters either, constantly lording it over their heads that she was the only mage of the girls.

How wrong she was about that. In fact, Ynya seemed to be the least capable mage of any of her sisters, even her youngest who shouldn't have bloomed yet.

The realization of just how wrong she was gave her pause.

Chapter Six

Ynya hadn't realized until recently just how valuable learning to cope and think without her magic was. She survived numerous attempts on her life. She took down a concentration camp. She prevailed despite her innate magic, and that was a lesson she would not soon forget.

She reached deep into the pocket of her dress, gripping the three earrings in her palm. She squeezed tight, impressing the three circles into her hand like she had done dozens of times trekking across the Gods-forsaken land of the Skarfanes.

I will not forget, and I will not give up.

"Meki, tell me about life here." Synol finally broke the silence.

Ynya was glad Synol said something. She was about to herself. The oppressive silence gave her too much of an excuse for her mind to wander, when she should be focused on getting her sisters out of this predicament.

"Oh, it's wonderful! "Meki replied in her high-pitched sweet little-girl voice. "Mother treats me so very well. We play games, and learn about magic, and we have so much fun."

Ynya chimed in, unable to allow Meki to keep calling the evil Frost Queen 'mother'. "Do you remember our *real* mother?" Ynya's emotions vacillated between two extremes. She wavered between crying for joy that her sisters were finally together or being furious that Meki was so far away and calling the bitch of a queen her mother.

Meki didn't reply, but there was a slight hitch in her next skip that betrayed the internal clock driving everything here.

Ynya felt the constant frost magic emanating from Meki dip slightly at the same time.

Meki corrected her next skip. "My previous life is in the past. I'm with Mother now and she gives me everything I need. I learn from her, and she helps me uncover my true power."

"And you use that power to shoot ice at your sisters? Maybe she's not teaching you proper manners. Maybe you should remember your *real* mother and what she sacrificed to keep you safe." Ynya regretted her retort the second it poured out of her mouth. They were words that a previous fire-driven Ynya would have said, not the one that walked through the camp of the Frost Queen. Not the one that had seen what she had seen thus far in her short life.

Meki whirled, her face scrunched up and beet-red. Dozens of ice spikes materialized out of the air as they flew towards Ynya.

Before hitting her, however, the spikes shattered into a million pieces, pelting Ynya's face with a dusting of snow and small ice balls as they lost momentum in the frigid air.

A gust of wind surged, picking up Meki and throwing her back a dozen feet onto her back. She grunted as she hit the ground. A large ice ball coalesced around her, freezing her to the ground.

The little girl screamed, frustrated and angry while she struggled to free herself from her newfound prison.

Behind Ynya, the Frost Queen's voice rang out in clear, unobstructed clarity.

"My dear girl, you allowed your temper to get the better of you once again. You must always be vigilant when you are in the midst of your enemy, for they will not be as patient with your mistakes as I."

Ynya winced at the sound of the Queen's voice.

The ice ball surrounding Meki shattered, and Meki lay on her back, sobbing.

The Frost Queen rushed forward and scooped up Meki in her arms, holding her to her breast and looking down at the eight-year-old child with the mass of red hair.

"Be still, little one. You learned a lesson today that will keep you alive someday."

Chapter Seven

The Frost Queen held Meki's hand the rest of the trek through the camp and up to the large gate in the side of the mountain.

Occasionally, Meki would look back at the group with a confused and panicked look on her face. Ynya always replied with as warm a smile as she could muster, given the situation.

There was no point in being mad at the little girl. *Eight-year-olds are barely in control of their emotions, let alone ones forced to live with despicable adults.*

Finny never once broke her gaze from whatever it was inside the mountain that had her so entranced. She now looked down at the ground a little bit, though it could have just been her watching Meki's little feet patter along the well-worn cobble road that lead into the Queen's castle lair.

Ynya looked up at the looming rock wall, entirely flabbergasted at the sheer size of the structure.

A biting shiver ran down her spine. She'd spent her entire life living just south of the Skarfanes, and had even hiked to the top a couple times with her father, but those were small hills compared to this mountain. They hadn't seemed like it at the time, but now she was older and wiser. Now, she had seen more of the world.

Ynya understood just how isolated her little fishing village of Marsfjord was, and how naive she had been. Her simple life of fishing and exploring had been turned upside down in one violent attack. She'd been thrust into the harsh reality of the world despite her reluctance to ever grow up.

She hoped she would be ready to deal the retaliating strike when the time came. She had already hesitated once already when presented with the perfect opportunity, and now she had her magic taken from her again and they were trapped.

Again.

She scanned up, taking in the dozen landings dotting the cliff face, and hundreds of smaller holes cut in the rock.

Her gaze stopped as she noticed the ice spikes. Her eyes narrowed and her mind reeled as she took in the horror of what had to be the ultimate torture from the Frost Queen.

Dotted around the top-most landing were spikes of ice protruding out from the wall. Atop each seemed to be the disfigured flesh of a tortured person.

Ynya's stomach soured and she tried to look away, horrified by the ghastly way those people had been treated. Still, she thought she saw movement through the light snowfall above her, so she tried to look closer.

She blinked, as a snowflake hit her upturned eyeball.

She squinted, trying to get a better look. Sure enough, each one of those people had not only been impaled by a spike through their torso, but each one of them flailed their arms and legs. Their mouths worked, screaming for their lives, though she couldn't hear them from this distance.

"They are quite alive, I assure you."

Ynya turned to come face to face with the Frost Queen. The two women were the same height, making them meet at eye level. It was a discomforting feeling having her so close. Every part of her cried out to shrink back, to shy away from being this close. Her stomach wrenched but she stood firm. She had to get to know her enemy before formulating a plan of escape.

Given how much she hated this woman, she wouldn't give her the satisfaction of talking directly to her. Ynya broke their stare-down first, turning to step closer to Finny.

"They scream all they want, but the wind drowns out their voices," the Queen said.

Beside Ynya, Synol asked the question they were all wondering. "How...how long have they been there?"

The Queen cocked her head to the side, like she was recalling a memory. "Now that you mention it, one of them has been there for over a hundred years. Perhaps she has learned her lesson and is ready to come down."

The Frost Queen smirked and turned. "Come now, we can't keep Baro waiting!"

***

The Queen led them inside, her metal-tipped shoes sounding on the stone floor with each step.

Clink clink clink!

Every dozen feet another soldier in white-dyed armor snapped to attention as she walked past. The Frost Queen certainly commanded respect, regardless of how she obtained it.

If Ynya had been younger, she might have been impressed by the deference the men took to their female queen. But if there was one lesson Ynya learned, it was that the ends did not justify the means. The respect the Queen commanded had been obtained through torture and threats, rather than benevolent leadership. She didn't deserve any of the respect they gave her.

She deserved to be devoured for all eternity by the Gods Below.

May the Raven ink your name early.

The group made their way up a long flight of stairs off the main hall and up to a spacious banquet hall.

Despite being carved into a mountain, the entire structure felt like a palace rather than a cave. Huge carved granite pillars supported the massive arched ceiling above them. Lamps teeming with glowing orbs hung on thick chains, bathing the whole room in a soft, blueish glow that reminded Ynya of the dim haze before sunup.

Regardless, it was effective in turning this cave-like interior into a somewhat welcome home.

Ornate tapestries hung from the wall. One of them alone would be large enough to cover her previous house in Marsfjord. Each must have weighed an incredible amount.

Each tapestry depicted the Frost Queen standing triumphant over some kind of battlefield. One was an icy terrain, another contained a black castle surrounded by thick woods.

Yet another pictured the Frost Queen holding a large sword over the slain body of another dark-skinned white-haired woman. All around them, bodies littered the ground on the large open plain. The foreign landscape comprised of an alien red rock, with gnarled trees rimming the outskirts of the battlefield. It was like something from a tale of old.

Distant memories of a tale her mother told her when she was a child tugged at her mind, but Ynya couldn't remember any specifics.

Something about the red rocks awash with blood...

"Do you like that one?" The Frost Queen sidled up to Ynya, startling her from her reverie. "That one is my greatest achievement, my largest victory."

The Queen took a few steps closer to the tapestry, squinting at the bloodied sword in her still-life hand. "Maegan Fields is a place far to the south, not a place you would have ever seen, being trapped up here in the north for so long, I suppose everyone forgot it existed."

Meki spoke up, startling Ynya. "Mother says she's going to take me to see Maegan Fields one day. She says it's even more beautiful in person than you can possibly imagine."

Ynya narrowed her eyes at her youngest sister. "She said that, huh?"

Meki hopped on the balls of her feet, though she slowed her pace when she noticed Ynya staring her down. "Yup! And we're going to go visit where she grew up and it will be all lush and green and full of trees and once we do that she will become Queen of the entire world!"

Ynya chanced a quick glance at the Queen, who watched Meki with a solemn look on her face. Ynya darted her eyes back to Meki before the Queen noticed.

"Lush and green?" Ynya still hadn't spoken directly to the Queen, and she didn't know that she would ever do that. Right now the only three people that mattered in this room were her sisters. She would focus on them, focus on what was important in her life. She hoped that by engaging Meki in conversation she might be able to remind the little girl what life had been like before the murderous hand of the Queen took everything from them.

Ynya's arm twitched, reminding her that she would rather punch the woman than ask about her childhood, but without any sort of access to magic at the moment, there wasn't much Ynya could do until she got the lay of the castle and figured out a way to exploit the Queen's weaknesses.

The Queen didn't take her eyes off of Meki, but replied anyway. "It's far to the south, past the Feond. You've most likely never heard of it, given your back-water upbringing. Such a shame that you had not been brought up in a better environment with me to guide your development."

Ynya didn't miss the fact that the Queen's gaze lingered on the woman beneath her sword, the one whose blood coated the blade.

Chapter Eight

Breakfast was served and it was the most delicious thing Ynya had ever tasted.

Synol wouldn't stop glaring at her the entire meal.

"What?" Ynya asked.

Synol looked away. "Nothing." She picked up her fork and moved her potatoes around on her plate again.

It was pretty clear Synol wasn't going to eat anything, but Ynya was famished, and at the very least she had to admit the food was well-made and delicious.

Besides, if the Queen wanted them dead, they would be dead already. Regardless of her tyrannical nature, the Queen had seemed to treat Meki well, even if she had trained her to call her mother.

Plus, Ynya hoped to lower the Queen's defenses by acting like she was at least partly all right with being trapped here. Ynya needed to learn a little more about their illustrious Queen of the North, but still refused to give her the satisfaction of addressing her directly. Instead, she asked Meki a question.

"So, Meki, how many new spells have you learned? You are incredibly young to be learning so many new things like this."

Meki's eyes got big and bright once again and she dropped her fork to the plate to talk. But just as she was about say something, the Queen cleared her throat.

Immediately, Meki's eyes narrowed and she closed her mouth. She picked her fork back up and turned to look at Ynya.

Despite the jovial look just a moment ago, Meki's entire countenance changed. Instead of the bright-eyed youth she'd been to Ynya all these years, her face now had a cold, hard look to it.

"I am a frost mage, and I have learned to unlock my full potential."

That was when Ynya noticed a wavering of magic between Meki and the Queen. It was barely perceptible, and only lasted a fraction of a second, but was distinct enough for Synol to turn her head in their direction.

Ynya speared another potato with her fork, stuffing it into her mouth. She spoke and chewed at the same time. "And what is your full potential?"

Meki glanced at the Queen, then back to Ynya. "I'm still learning that."

Ynya nodded. "That's good to hear. We all have a lot of potential built within us when we are born. We can do great and we can do terrible things."

Synol kicked her under the table, followed by a glare that should have set her on fire.

Ynya glared back even more fiercely, then looked across the table at her youngest sister.

Part of her brain yelled at her to stop digging the hole she was in. She knew she should, but something about this felt like the right thing to do. She'd tried to go in hands blazing before, she'd tried that and failed too many times. Regardless, she wasn't the type to just do nothing at all. She had to act, she had to try something, and following around the Frost Queen through a tour of her house wasn't getting them any closer to escaping.

Ynya needed to push. She needed to prod. She needed to get a reaction out of the Queen, so she would finally expose some kind of weakness. The only thing she'd done was think about killing the Queen, and got her magic taken away because of it. It wasn't much, but at least it was the start of building a profile about the enemy.

Ynya continued. "What is important is what we choose to do with those abilities." She gestured around the table, pointing at each of her sisters in turn. "Before a couple months ago, I had no idea that my sisters had access to magic. Now, here we are, two months later and we have all manner of magic users gathered together around the table."

Ynya put her fork down and stood. Her stomach was in knots, and the icy glare from Synol bore into the back of her head, but she ignored those feelings, pushing them down deep in order to allow the righteous anger she'd been holding on to for so long to rise to the surface once again.

She almost felt her familiar heat rise with her anger, but it was still just out of reach.

So close, but so far.

"Only, some of us don't have access to that magic right now because perhaps another person at this table is too scared of what they will do with that magic."

Ynya looked at Meki, but not before glancing at the Queen, who chewed slowly. "I just think that it's important to

45

look at what we do with our magic. Simply having magic is a blessing from the Gods Above, but what we choose to do with that magic is what defines us. Taking others' magic without their permission and using your own magic to force them to do what you want is one thing you can do with your magic, but there are other things you can do."

Ynya's heart pounded in her chest and in her temples.

What am I doing? She was far beyond poking and prodding, but her mouth just wouldn't stop spewing words.

She turned to the rest of the table, glancing at Finny across from her and Synol to her side. "I just think that we all need to remember that how we act matters, don't you agree?"

Ynya turned toward the Queen, who, surprisingly, wore a smile across her face.

"I like you, Ynya. I really do. I know you might think I'm some kind of tyrant, and perhaps I am, but the simple fact is that you haven't seen the things I have in my life."

The Queen stood, grabbed the side of her shirt and lifted, exposing her side. A thick scar ran across her middle, starting from her navel and wrapping halfway around her back. "My own father did this to me, nearly cut me in half with his large axe. It was only through the bravery of my brother that I'm alive today. He gave his life so that I might live."

She put down her shirt and put a leather boot on the table, lifting up her skirt to show off an oddly smooth and silvery patch of skin on her lower left leg. "I was burned here too, and I have many other scars I could show off if you truly are curious."

She dropped her skirt and put her foot back down on the cold stone floor.

"I have lived a very long time, Ynya, and I have seen many things that would curdle your stomach. Perhaps I am a tyrant, but I'm a tyrant on a mission and I will obtain what I seek. All I am trying to do is get back what is mine, I assume you can understand that notion?"

The Queen gestured to Ynya's other sisters. "You have killed hundreds of my soldiers in order to recover your own sisters, but you begrudge me doing the same to return back to my homeland? All I want is to return home after being forced away. You of all people should understand that sentiment, no? We are not so different when it comes down to what we are willing to do to return home with our family."

The Queen pursed her lips and stared Ynya down for what seemed like an eternity.

Terror surged through Ynya.

This might be it. Over before it began.

Ynya had already said too much, and she was going to be killed for it.

Or worse, put on one of those ice spikes.

The Queen's eyes narrowed, and she brought up her hand.

Ynya tensed as magic swirled around the Queen.

The Queen snapped her fingers.

Inside her chest, Ynya's magic burst forward, pushing heat into her extremities with a shivering tingle.

"You want your magic back? Fine. I'm not afraid of you in the slightest. I am quite curious to see what you choose to do with it."

Chapter Nine

Ynya didn't move.
No one did.

The moment stretched on for what seemed an age before the Queen finally huffed, turned to Meki, and spoke. "Time for you to train, little one."

Meki stood, her wide eyes never leaving Ynya. Meki's little lip trembled ever so slightly, or at least Ynya hoped that was what she saw.

Ynya saw easily through the bluster in her little sister. Meki was still a little girl taken from her mother too young and now controlled by an evil monster to be used for her own needs.

As Meki turned to follow the Queen, Ynya returned a warm smile. She smiled until Meki finally broke the gaze and followed the Queen out of the room.

Ynya couldn't describe it, but she thought she saw something in those eyes. She thought she saw her old sister for a moment.

"What about us?" Ynya asked before the Queen left the spacious dining room.

The Queen stopped, turning her head back slightly, but still not far enough to look at any of them.

"As I told you before, you are guests in my home. Feel free to roam around, visit old friends, or take a nap. I do have activities planned for everyone, so I would recommend filling your stomachs and resting as much as you can. It's not all dinner parties and naps here. Things have been set in motion and your late arrival has me scrambling to get certain things done, so you will have to excuse me for leaving in the middle of a meal."

With that, she left, Meki in tow.

Ynya fell back into her seat, relishing her missing fire. All the tension built up in her shoulders and neck from mouthing off to the Queen released, leaving her jittery and jumpy. She wanted to punch something to get out her nerves.

I can't believe I did that!

Synol let out an exasperated breath.

Ynya looked at Finny, whose face had a curious and frightened expression. "Are you okay, Finny?"

Finny looked back at Ynya. "Yes, why would I not be?"

"Because the Frost Queen took our magic."

Finny scrunched up her eyebrows. "No, she did not. I had access to my magic the entire time."

Ynya stood, putting her hands on the table. Now that her fire was back, her temper flared with it.

"You had access to your magic this entire time?"

Finny nodded, her face devoid of any regret. "Of course. I felt her take yours and Synol's but she didn't take mine."

Ynya fisted her hands, but didn't quite know what to do with them. She wasn't really mad at Finny, it wasn't her fault.

Maybe the Queen hadn't felt threatened by Finny, but had by Synol?

That's at least something.

Ynya also wondered if there was some kind of game the Queen was playing. By favoring one sister over the other, or treating them differently, she might successfully drive a wedge between them that could fester.

Ynya dropped all frustration from her mind. No matter how much any of them got on each other's nerves, she couldn't allow doubt to keep them apart. Too much was at stake, and the Queen held all the power right now.

Ynya needed to pay attention.

Smoke, not fire.

"So, what is the plan?"

Synol glanced around. "Don't you think there would be a better place to discuss this?"

Ynya looked around. No one else was in the room that she could see. "Why not? We're alone."

Synol huffed, her eyes narrowing. "Ynya, no one in royalty is ever *truly* alone. I guarantee you that behind each of those tapestries are listening locations where she has people writing down everything we discuss."

Synol turned and pointed to the two doors on one wall. "There are soldiers stationed just outside of the room, and don't forget there are the servants that brought us the food. They are probably at their door right now, listening."

Ynya looked around at the various doors and tapestries, finally realizing what Synol was talking about. Part of her didn't care, though.

"So what? It doesn't matter, anyway. If what you say is true, then she's going to have us watched every second of the day, so we won't have any privacy. If that's the case, then why worry about something we can't control? We might as well just be honest with each other because otherwise we're going to have to sneak around and whisper to say hello in the morning."

Ynya sat back down and grabbed a biscuit off her plate. Breaking off a piece, she turned back to Finny. "Do you know why she didn't take your magic?"

Synol grabbed the biscuit from Ynya and tossed it back onto the plate. "You think this is a game?"

Ynya dropped the little bit of biscuit from her hand and stood again, getting dangerously close to Synol's scrunched face.

They were both clearly angry, but Ynya didn't rightly care right now. "Yes, it's a game that you taught me to play, remember?"

Ynya leaned closer, nose to nose with Synol. Despite her desire to keep petty squabbles to a minimum, Synol just had a way about her that got under Ynya's skin far too easily.

"Aren't I supposed to say things without saying them? Didn't I do that with her just now by talking to *Meki* rather than *her*? I thought you would be proud that I'm learning from you and trying new things."

Ynya pointed to the tapestry. "If we are truly guests like she says, then let's act like guests. Let's eat, wander around, explore, and take in the sights. Sure, she's probably going to have us followed the whole time, but there isn't much we can do about that, can we? We can argue like we did in the past, or we can find out more about this place and what is going on."

Ynya sat back down in her chair, grabbed the biscuit and shoved half of it into her mouth.

She was done arguing. It was time to do something.

Synol huffed, balled up her fists like she was going to hit

something, but then turned and stormed away, her boots clomping on the stone.

Finny and Ynya glanced at each other for a moment before Finny smiled. "I like it when the two of you pretend to fight. It's cute."

"We're not pretending!" Synol shouted from across the room.

Ynya spoke with her mouth full. "She's just jealous that *I* got our magic back from the Queen instead of her."

Ynya munched on her biscuit for a bit longer, wishing she hadn't bit off so much.

Synol tromped around behind her, but Ynya gave her no mind. Synol would calm down once the conversation started up again.

Finny sat back down on her chair with a melancholy look about her. She picked up her goblet and drained it in one gulp, then set it back down on the table probably harder than she expected, resulting in the goblet falling over, rolling off the table, and hitting the stone floor.

As it hit the floor, it rang out with a combination of dull thud and high-pitched ping.

Faster than Ynya'd ever seen her move, Finny shot out of her chair, grabbed the goblet with one hand, sat back down in her chair, and placed the goblet back where it should have been.

She'd managed to do the motion in the time between the goblet's first and second bounce, which was no small feat.

"You caught it too late, now the goblet is forever marred by the floor." Ynya replied.

Finny huffed, a small smile gracing her downturned lips. "Maybe I allowed it to be damaged so that it wasn't perfect. Maybe now that it has some damage to it, it will be more real.

Now it has a story it can tell other goblets, about how it survived a fall off a table and came away slightly damaged but still usable."

Synol chimed in. "Finny, that was incredibly fast. How did you do that?"

Finny shrugged, adjusting the angle of the goblet on the table before her. A small flat dent on the lip betrayed the fact that the goblet had been dropped. "It's all part of the modifications they did to me while I was at Reyoarfjell."

The mention of the concentration camp precursed silence in the room. All three girls pursed their lips and concentrated on looking at their own plates for a while.

It wasn't something they discussed, but they had all been changed drastically by that place, Finny more than the other two. What she had gone through was unquestioningly the worst thing any person should have to go through, and her being so young made it all the worse.

No child should know that the world is bad enough to do that to someone.

But the unspoken pall in the room made Ynya think about the physical changes to Finny. She now had the ability to change into a beast and roam the wilderness in bounds rather than two human legs. She was part human and part beast.

Ynya didn't know which part Finny associated herself with more, but it wasn't something she wanted to ask.

Realizing the direction her thoughts were headed, Ynya forced herself to rout that line of thinking from her head and focus instead on the goblet.

Ynya supposed if Finny had wanted to, she could have caught that thing and had it placed back before anyone had noticed.

The fact that she had allowed it to hit the floor once before grabbing it was the important thing here.

Finny tapped her fingernail on the metal goblet, listening to the ring through the large room.

Synol giggled.

Ynya looked over at her oldest sister, shocked that a giggle had come from her. Synol was usually so uptight and put together that a giggle wasn't something she expected.

The whole notion made Ynya want to giggle, but she managed to keep her composure in check.

Though it never got easier, as Synol replied by clinking her fingernail on her goblet.

Finny sighed.

Ynya noticed. "Finny, what's wrong?"

Finny looked up. "I haven't been completely honest with you two."

Chapter Ten

Ynya turned, catching Synol's concerned expression.
"Why? What's wrong?" Synol asked.

Finny eyed both sisters in turn then back down to her plate. "The reason she didn't take my magic is because she controls it. When I'm near her, something about my training and the way my magic was manipulated came out. I have no control over my magic when I'm near her, so I wasn't a threat to her at all. It's like all of the wind magic changes into something else when I'm around her."

Finny looked back across the table, this time with tears in her eyes and a horrified look on her face. It was the most emotion Ynya had seen on her sister since they had reconnected weeks ago. Usually the poor girl was so careful and matter of fact.

"The magic I had before I went to Reyoarfjell is still mine, but that was just basic wind magic that Mama taught me to use. The magics they pulled out of me at Reyoarfjell are much more powerful, and there are some you haven't seen before, some I haven't even tried yet. I feel them in there but I'm too afraid to use them. I can't access them when I'm like this, though. I don't know how to explain it better."

Finny picked up her goblet once again, running her thumb across the flattened part of the metal that had recently hit the floor. In an absent-minded move, she attempted to drink from the goblet, but realizing there was nothing in there, she hurled the goblet across the room with such ferocity that it didn't bounce off the stone wall. Instead, it crumpled near-to-flat and stuck for a split second before falling.

Both Ynya and Synol stared at the flattened goblet.

"I'm constantly at war. I don't know which of my selves I should focus on, or if I should embrace them both. Each side of me wars against the other and the only stable thing I have in my life right now is you.

"One side wants me to remain, the other wants me to move on, but I don't think I can live like this forever. Sooner or later I'm going to have to choose to embrace one side or the other. One day, I may not be the same Finny that you know. I don't want to, but I might have to. I don't think I have a choice because it's all just too much to handle right now."

Finny buried her face in her hands and fell onto the table.

Ynya hadn't seen Finny cry once since they found her in Reyoarfjell. It was a worrying thing to see her with tears in her eyes and emotion across her face. Ynya wondered if the monster inside of Finny had taken over completely.

But something else was going on inside of the poor girl. Something dark and sinister had clearly been brewing since they had escaped Reyoarfjell. Whatever it was, she had done a good job of hiding it from her sisters. Now that Ynya knew about it, she could do something to help.

Ynya turned to address Synol, and ask if she wanted to step outside into the hallway, to discuss this situation with Finny, but before she could speak, Finny had lifted her head and addressed the room again.

This time, all emotion was gone from her voice. She spoke in a careful monotone, like she was reciting a passage of scripture she hadn't wanted to memorize and deliver in front of a crowd.

"There is one more thing I have to tell you."

Finny pointed at the floor to the side of the table. "I'm not the only one who came from that place. Another is trapped down there and calls to me. I hear him howling in my head. Every step we've taken closer to the castle he's been getting louder and louder.

"I've been keeping it from you, and for that I'm sorry, but I wanted you to know before we go and see him. I know the first thing you are going to say is that we shouldn't go, but I'm not asking you, I'm telling you. I have to go see him."

Synol ran around the table to hold her sister.

Ynya stood and watched the two of them, feeling horrible that she hadn't noticed this about Finny sooner.

"What do you mean going to see him?"

Finny turned, looking through the floor. "He's down there, the other one of me. He came from that place before I did. He was the first one that they managed to convert to...to whatever it is that I am, only he isn't the same. He can't change like I can, I know that much.

"Now that we are closer, we can talk through our minds. Not whole sentences, but feelings. We sense each other and I know exactly where he is. He's waiting for me, trapped and alone, and I need to go find him. I need to let him know that he's not alone."

Ynya and Synol stared at each other, trying to have a silent conversation of their own. Neither seemed to know what to say.

Ynya's mind raced. Finny was clearly talking about her beast form that she took to roam around at night. Maybe this explained why she had been out for so long last night. Normally she was only out for short bits of time, scouting, possibly eating.

Hunting.

But she always came back, and she was always her, the proper Finny.

Though by the sounds of it, Finny was more than just what she appeared to be. Perhaps the Translator had changed Finny more than Ynya thought. Perhaps Finny would never be the sweet, loving, literal girl she'd always been. Maybe her new life with dual forms changed her more than Ynya had realized.

Finally, Synol squeezed Finny. "I will support you no matter what, Finny. Ynya and I both will."

Ynya sat back down. "We are family. That is what we are, and nothing the Queen does to us will change that, Finny. No matter what is going on in your life, we are here for you. Even if we don't fully understand what you're going through, we will be by your side to help where we can. Just tell us if anything is going on with you so we know."

Ynya sighed. "I had no idea this other beast was in your head. I wish you would have told us so we can help. Maybe there is a way to block his voice?"

Finny looked up, wiping tears off her cheeks which shaking her head. "I don't want him out of my head, that's the worst part. I *need* to go see him. I need to talk to him, find out why he's been calling and crying for me. I'm not scared of him, I'm more scared for him. I just need to go see him, but I'm also worried about coming face to face with him. I know it doesn't make any sense."

Ynya balled up her fists, the anger flowing through her once again. This time it wasn't directed at her sisters. This time it was the familiar focused rage that made her blood boil and her mind centered.

Of course it made sense. Everyone experienced that uniquely human emotion of not wanting to do something, but knowing you had to do anyway.

Ynya relished the heat once again. She had missed it for the short time the Queen had taken it from her. She dug her fingernails into her palms. "Finny, would it help if we went down there with you?"

Chapter Eleven

᠅

"So, you wish to visit our newest monster of the deep?" A woman from the doorway replied.

The female voice was both familiar and terrifying, setting Ynya's hairs on the back of her neck on edge.

The voice had a casual edge to it that could only come from a Skarmyord, one of the Frost Queen's elite guards who had been through the entire round of torture and reprogramming offered by Reyoarfjell.

Ynya whirled around to stare at the woman in black leaning against the doorway. She wore a sinister smirk on her angular, narrow face, and her piercing eyes instantly made Ynya remember the night she had demonstrated her power to Ynya on the top of the carriage.

It was the night that Ynya had managed to finally escape her clutches and kill the other Skarmyord.

Ynya scowled and built up energy in her hands. "Captain Nora. I was wondering when you'd show up again."

Behind her, Synol pulled magic in as well.

The woman in black pulled a small silver dagger from her sheath and twirled it around her fingers. "Do you really want your magic taken from you so soon after getting it back? I am to be your escort through the castle so you may want to keep your forked tongue behind your teeth. Or do you want to be taught another lesson in humility?"

Nora whirled the blade once more and re-sheathed it, folding her arms in front of her. Her face took on a hard, pained expression, one of deadly sincerity. "You can try attacking, but anything you do to me is nothing compared to the punishment I'll obtain from the Queen, so if you are going to kill me, make sure you do it swiftly and completely so there is nothing more she can punish."

Ynya imagined the woman in black impaled on the ice spikes at the top of the mountain. She wasn't sure why the thought came into her head, but it felt more like a memory than a dream. A chill ran down Ynya's spine.

Ynya dropped her fire, and felt Synol let go of her earth magic as well. Finny hadn't flared any magic.

"We don't need a babysitter," Ynya said, grabbing her chair and plunking down into it.

"It's not a request," the elite guard answered coolly, checking her fingernails.

Ynya folded her arms and glared at the Skarmyord.

Ever since the Warden had shown her the book containing her mother's entry into the concentration camp, there had been a question nagging the back of Ynya mind.

She decided to hold onto her verbal jabs for now. There might be a better time to bring it up. Despite needing to get her sisters safely out of this castle, she had questions, and this woman seemed like the right one to ask.

"Fine. If you're our escort, then show us the way. I assume you have to do whatever we want?"

Nora's eyes narrowed. "Within reason. There are a few rules you must follow."

Ynya huffed. "And what are those."

Nora paused before replying. "I think it might be more fun if you just stumble into them; more fun for me at least."

Ynya's typical anger flared, prodding for her to retort, but she clamped down the urge to mouth off and instead turned to Finny. "Well, you heard what the nice lady said. She will be happy to escort us down to see whoever it is that you need to see."

Captain Nora led them into the hallway, then back to the main staircase. Finny followed immediately behind the Skarmyord, with Synol behind her and Ynya at the rear.

On their way down the stairs, Synol nudged Ynya and whispered to her. "You think this is a good idea?"

Ynya shrugged. "It's *an* idea, and right now, we don't have anything else to work on. Why, you think we should be doing something else?"

Synol rolled her eyes. "I'm not talking about miss tight-pants over there, I'm talking about Meki. Shouldn't one of us be with her?"

Nora spoke up from the front of the pack. "When Her Majesty is training, no one is to disturb her. You will have to ask her if you can join in her training sessions, though I have a feeling you'll be a party to that soon enough."

Nora hadn't missed a single step through her entire spiel, garnering a frustrated look from Synol.

"Oh, yes, I can hear everything you say."

Ynya snapped back, the frustration palpable in her voice.

"I have no expectation of privacy, given how scared the Queen is of a bunch of young girls. It does surprise me just how much she's worried that we might have any freedom. Seems like she should feel more powerful given that we're in her own castle, or whatever this cave is. Oh, that reminds me."

Ynya turned to Synol, wrapping her arm around her sister's. "Do you remember that time when we were in the carriage and someone dragged us up to the roof to prove how powerful she was? Did you know that she actually helped me escape my bonds by taking me outside into the wind?"

Synol glared but Ynya was having too much fun. "If she hadn't taken me into the cold blowing wind, I would have never been able to shed enough heat to melt through the iron bonds. Had she just left me in the cabin instead of taking me out I would have never escaped. Maybe next time she won't feel the need to lord how big and strong she is in the face of her prisoners. It might make her feel powerful in the moment, but I don't forget, and will use any opportunity to prove just how wrong she was."

Nora stopped and whirled, her face a mixture of rage and singular intensity. She stared at Ynya for a long second before her face relaxed. "We should hurry, we don't want to keep the monster waiting for his girlfriend." She flashed a jocular expression and turned back down the stairs.

Ynya stewed at this for a while, wanting to retort, but nothing really came to her. The last thing she wanted to do was insult Finny, who was the whole reason they were following this horrible woman.

Nora had incredible control of her emotions.

Of course she would, she'd been alive for a long time and had been through the concentration camp known as Reyoarf-

jell to train to become a Skarmyord, the elite guard of the Frost
Queen.

The memory of the books with her mother's registration
had been at the forefront of Ynya's mind ever since she had
seen them. The fact that Nora Oblique had been the name
right next to her own mother's, and she now had a Skarmyord
with the first name of Nora seemed like too much of a coin-
cidence.

Ynya wasn't entirely sure how much she truly wanted to
know one way or the other. If the woman was her aunt, did
that change anything? She clearly had no sense of moral oblig-
ation when it came to family. She was a soldier for the Frost
Queen and nothing more. Maybe Ynya could try a different
tack to get a reaction out of Nora.

Ynya's heart pounded against her ribs. She knew she was
pushing the woman hard, but she needed to. She needed to
elicit a guttural reaction to see how far she could push her. If
they weren't going to tell her what her rules were, then she had
no choice but to seek them out of her own accord. That way,
when she was punished, at least she would have done something worthy of the punishment.

"Captain Nora Oblique? Sister of my mother, Talia
Oblique? How old are you, exactly? Mama never spoke of a
sister, though after meeting you I think I know why. She also
didn't tell us just how old you all are. Are you over one
hundred? If so, I'm rather impressed, because I don't see much
drooping like most of the ancient shriveled grandmas you
slaughtered."

Lub-dub.

Ynya's heart seemed to slow, and her vision focused on the
placement of the woman's next footstep. Nora's foot was

angled out slightly, a tell-tale sign of the sort of thing Ynya had been pushing her to perform.

Nora turned and pulled her dagger, throwing it in one fast motion.

Anticipating the reaction, Ynya jumped to the side, pushing Synol away from her. Ynya went one way, with Synol the other, the dagger narrowly missing both of them as it sailed past and hit the stone wall behind them with a resounding metallic *clang*.

The entire scene was surreal. Ynya's heart pounded in her chest as she sprung to her feet, reading for a fight.

Nora's face hardened and she took a step toward the girls, but Finny was in front of her so fast Ynya had to blink to believe it. Five knife-sharp talons from Finny's now-blackened hand dug into the Skarmyord's chest plate.

"I would leave my sisters alone if you don't want your heart ripped out. You are supposed to be escorting us, not fighting with us."

Nora's gaze never left Ynya's but she huffed and spat on the ground.

"Get your filthy claws off me, dog."

Finny growled, a guttural, feral sound that Ynya had heard before on the wind late at night while she couldn't sleep. A deep chill settled in the back of her head, dissipating through her scalp.

"Finny. She's not worth it. We learned what we needed to anyway."

Finny growled once again, but Nora took the first step back, detaching her leather breastplate from Finny's claws.

Ynya took a couple steps forward to stand directly in front of the Skarmyord. She wrapped her arm around her younger sister, and hugged. "Thank you Finny. I appreciate you looking out for our little family."

Synol chimed in, having just picked herself up off the floor.

"So you are our aunt, I guess that fact has been established. Anything else we should know?"

Nora huffed and turned. "I have all the family I need."

Chapter Twelve

The rest of the trip down the stairs was silent. They went right to the main floor that led out to the plains and the standing army of the Queen.

Seeing the place for the second time, Ynya was able to concentrate more on the details than she had when she was being led in by the Frost Queen earlier that day.

Two staircases flanked opposite sides of the massive cave, with towering pillars supporting the immense rock ceiling above them. The expansive room was large enough that hundreds of soldiers could easily stand at attention in here, possibly a thousand if needed. It was chilly in the space, but nowhere near as cold as outside.

The drone of the wind was ever-present no matter where she had been in the castle, but it was definitely more pronounced in here. The constant song of the north, the ebb and flow of the wind, howled along to the other activity that continued to support the Queen's empire.

Spaced along the outside of the cave were dozens of doorways leading to stables, blacksmiths, cobblers, and other assorted vendors. Well over a hundred tradesmen hammered, cut, and filed their various crafts, but each one did so to some unseen beat of nature.

Lub-dub. Lub-dub.

Ynya's heart pounded in her chest. Each step down the stairs matching her heart's cadence.

She hated the feeling that she was following some unseen mandate from the Queen. It was as intrusive as it was rhythmic, and the fiery rage inside of her lashed out, refusing to follow the unseen beat.

Ynya skipped a step, falling out of line with the never-ending silent pulse, and concentrated inward, willing her heart to slow slightly out of pace from the magic surrounding her.

Her heart didn't respond, at least not at first.

She concentrated really hard, forcing her heart to beat differently. A growing hardness in her chest weighed her down, pulling her back into the familiar groove of the Queens magic.

Regardless, she pushed harder, focusing her mind inward, rather than outward on her steps.

Lub-dub, lub-dub.

Ynya pushed harder, like she was using a muscle for the first time. Forcing her heart to beat erratically was a futile effort, but it was one she wanted to try, one that she needed to interrupt. She couldn't fathom being locked in time with every other man and woman under the Queen's spell. She wanted, no, she *needed* to break free and forge her own path.

She tried again, this time focusing even more inward. Her magic swelled at the reaction, adding in heat and a little bit of hardness–

Lub——dub.

For one glorious moment in time, Ynya had bucked the Queen's overall mandate and had forced herself to go against the grain. It was exhilarating, and terrifying, and made her weak in the chest. Her weak knees nearly gave out and she stumbled to the side.

I skipped the beat!

Synol grabbed her arm to steady her. "Are you all right?"

Ynya nodded, but she would not forget that brief moment of exhilaration she felt by not being in time with the Queen's magic.

My heart actually skipped a beat!

Despite their lot in life, being under the thumb of the Queen, Ynya felt a small thread of hope. She had broken out of the Queen's magic for an exhilarating moment. That meant there was hope, and hope was enough for now.

Synol helped her get back into line and catch up with the two who had started across the large expansive room.

In the back of the massive castle foyer, between the stairs leading up, was an immense staircase leading down.

Nora led them down deep into the earth. The stairs were wide enough that half a dozen horses could ride side-by-side with ease, and tall enough that, well, Ynya didn't know of any animals that were taller than a frost bear on its hind-legs, but three bears stacked on top of each other wouldn't be tall enough to hit their heads.

"Into the depths of hell." Nora stated, before sighing under her breath and descending the stairs.

Ynya glanced at Finny, who now held hands with Synol. "You ready?"

Finny's gaze was locked onto to a spot down and to the left.

She nodded to the affirmative, her lips set. "Yes. I must do this."

Every step down increased the smell. It became clear to Ynya that this was where they stabled all the animals.

Hundreds of horses, sheep, and other animals were locked in pens down here in the depths.

She supposed it was an effective means to keep animals safe from the howling winds of the outside, but the work involved to carve out such a massive cave system had to have been draining.

Then again, the Queen didn't have to do the work, she just tortured her subjects until they did it for her.

Lub-dub.

There was no escaping the Queen's mandates for her subjects. The ease at which Ynya fell back into the Queen's all-encompassing beat was testament to that.

The room was at least four times the size of the one upstairs, though the ceiling was significantly lower.

Nora turned left and led them past the sheep pens and a couple dog kennels before turning down a narrow hallway on the left wall. She stopped, coming to a thick iron door with a single viewing window at eye-height.

Nora turned around. "Go ahead. It's waiting for you. I assume you and he have a lot to discuss."

Finny dropped Synol's hand and took two steps to stand in front of the door. She grabbed the handle and paused.

"Do you want one of us to go in there with you?" Synol asked.

Finny let out a slow breath, a tinge of sadness creeping into her face. "I—don't know yet. I've heard him calling for me for so long, I am not entirely sure what I'm here for."

"I don't hear anything now."

It was true. No sound came from the other side of the iron door.

Finny tapped her head with her middle finger. "He stopped once we started coming down the stairs. I hear him breathing in there."

Nora spoke up. "If it's any consolation, he's in a cage."

Ynya flashed a look at the Skarmyord, but Nora hadn't bothered looking up at any of them. She looked bored, leaning up against a wall and examining a speck of dirt under her fingernail.

"I better do it," Finny said. She paused for a second to flash a weak smile at her two older sisters before proceeding.

Rusty hinges squealed in anguish as Finny opened the door and disappeared into the blackness beyond.

A caustic, rotten, hot air blew out of the room, blasting Ynya in the face and blowing back her hair.

Her stomach lurched, threatening to upturn her recent breakfast onto the stone floor, but she clutched her middle, pinched her nose, and took a moment to calm herself before stepping thorough the doorway. Synol followed behind, looking fairly green herself.

Inside was terribly dark, and Ynya lit up a portion of her hair to bathe the room in a soft warm glow.

What she saw looked to be a mixture of the concentration camp's experiment room, and an animal cage.

In fact, that's exactly what it was.

A large iron cage with bars bolted through the floor and ceiling stood in the center, with a half-dozen tables, chairs, and desks surrounding the outside.

Every damn time, the victim is in the pen in the center while the tyrants ring the outside.

But inside the cage was just as horrifying.

A lone creature huddled in the center. Its skin was mottled black and grey, much like Finny's hands when she held back Nora from attacking Ynya. It hunched over on all fours, the black-ened skin pulled taut over a bony frame. Thick talons graced its hands and feet, and sharp spines protruded from its head and down along its back. Its cheekbones were hollow and sunken, with white cloudy eyes that seemed to glow in the low light.

It looked like a cross between a feral dog, a human, and a porcupine.

Synol gasped and ran out of the room.

Ynya turned to follow Synol, but the creature's eyes pulled her back.

Something about those eyes drew a second, more careful study from Ynya. They both stared back, unblinking in the darkness, but they didn't contain the expected feral look of a wild predator. No, what Ynya saw was recognition, and possibly compassion.

Flashes of snow shook Ynya's memory, but she couldn't quite place them. She allowed the memory to wash over her but it quickly dissipated before it stuck, eluding her for now.

A shudder ran down Ynya's spine, but try as she might, she couldn't take her gaze away from the beast.

It's almost like I know it, but how could that be?

It whimpered, raising a clawed paw to the cage and lowering it slowly.

Not thinking about it, Ynya replied with the same motion using her own hand. It was both scary and familiar. She didn't know which was the more prominent of the two emotions.

Ynya hadn't forgotten her first impression of seeing her sister strapped to the table.

Finny took a cautious step toward the cage.

"Be careful," Ynya called softly after her, finally breaking the gaze of the beast.

Finny turned her head toward Ynya. Her face had begun to take on the same transformation, with white eyes and taut, skeletal features. Her skin began to mottle, and Ynya noticed the hair on her head coalescing into thicker spines instead of soft, curly red hair.

Ynya pursed her lips, hardening her features to not betray what her mind wanted to do, which was scream and run from the sight.

She couldn't do that though, not for her sister who had gone through so much pain.

Finny's life had been a living hell since she had arrived at Reyoarfjell all these weeks ago, and neither Ynya nor Synol had been much help to her since they left. Maybe it explained why she had been so matter of fact, or hard sometimes. She was both her old self, as well as this new creature.

Finny had been fighting her own internal battle to determine who she was and how she fit into the world now that her soul had been ripped from her body and shoved into something new and unknown.

She was half-girl, half-monster, trying to figure out where she belonged. Ynya at least understood a part of that, growing up as the only magic wielder in a family.

Or at least that's what she had thought until she learned all of that was a ruse.

Regardless, it wouldn't be right for Ynya to panic in front of her sister.

Ynya nodded. "Go ahead, but be cautious. I just don't want you to get hurt. Call if you need me, even if it's just to hold your hand or bring you water."

Finny grunted, a guttural, low-pitched sound, and turned back toward the cage.

Ynya backed away, turning off her light and exiting through the door.

Finny and the beast needed some alone time.

Chapter Thirteen

❦

The three women stood in the hallway, each one trying to ignore the grunts and whines coming from the room.

A soldier came down the hallway, holding a steaming mug in his hand. He stopped when he noticed the three in the hallway.

Nora spoke up, leaping from the wall with an uncanny grace and speed. "Under order of the Queen herself, I am escorting a friend for your creature in there."

The man nodded and peered beyond them into the room. His eyes widened with understanding before turning and leaving.

"So, are we going to talk about this?" Ynya finally spoke up after the man had left.

Nora huffed, folding her arms and leaning against the wall once more. "Talk about what?"

"The fact that you are our aunt. Is is true? Is what the Warden told us true?"

Nora turned her head, staring down the hallway toward the kennels.

The rage returned in a flash. Ynya stepped in front of her, building up heat in her hands. She wanted answers, and now that Nora didn't have her special little dagger anymore, she would do anything to get those answers.

Synol grabbed Ynya's arm and pulled her back. "Ynya, perhaps we should worry about our sister rather than someone who doesn't want to admit she's part of the family."

Nora glared at Synol, turned, and walked out of the hallway. "I will be waiting for you when you are done."

Synol smiled broadly.

"What was that about?" Ynya asked.

Synol pursed her lips, trying to contain the devious look she now wore. "Just dropping the seed of familial guilt. Whatever it takes to break through her barrier."

Synol wore a strange expression on her face, like she knew something but didn't want anyone to know how pleased she was with herself over knowing the thing. It was infuriating beyond words.

"Oh Gods Above, Synol."

"What?"

"You look so much like Mama there. Like when father came home from his fishing trips and she would spend the day trying not to smile constantly. That's what you look like now, and given how much you look like her, it's getting a bit creepy."

Synol frowned, but didn't fully give her up whimsical look. "I think we can wear her down, but remember that the Queen is always watching us, so let's just be very careful with what we say near her for the time being."

Ynya nodded, looking around. "I think we're fairly safe here."

Synol nodded. "Yeah, I think Nora was supposed to be

here the whole time, which is one reason I jabbed at her. I wanted to get a reaction out of her."

"That's what I was doing on the staircase, and I think it worked."

Synol cocked her lips to the side. "Perhaps, but remember she's a hardened soldier, so reacting to anger-based situations and physically violent threats is what she's trained for. Reacting to emotional situations might make it tougher for her to keep up the facade she wears."

Synol scratched her chin, her eyes not leaving the place where Nora had just been. "Regardless, we just need to be careful."

A thought popped into Ynya's head. "Hand signals."

Synol looked at her with a quizzical look. "What?"

Ynya nodded, excitedly. "When we were caught by the Warden, he said he recognized we weren't soldiers coming in because we didn't use the proper hand signal. My guess is that they were forced to start using them based on something Mama did years ago. That's my theory anyway."

Ynya showed Synol the signal with her thumb and tapping her palm. "Like this. I learned it when I was sneaking around Reyoarfjell looking for you."

Synol's eyes lit up with understanding. "I like it, reminds me of the signals we used to use with Mama when we were young."

Ynya was confused. "Mama did these?"

Synol nodded. "You don't remember? She would use these to tell us to be quiet when we were about to say something inappropriate, or remind us to pray to the Gods Above, or, well, you remember, don't you?"

Ynya shook her head "I have no idea what you are talking about."

Synol furrowed her eyes. "Finny, Meki, and Mother used them from time to time to communicate."

"Wait, I remember when I stole old man Grindhill's chicken and he was giving mama a scolding about how she raised me, you kept doing a motion with your hand and chin."

"You mean like this?" Synol replicated the gesture.

"Yes! Just like that!"

Synol rolled her eyes. "That was for you to stop talking and let Mama handle it."

"But I didn't, I ended up yelling at him, stomping on his foot, and running away."

Synol pursed her lips. "Yes, and what happened? You got in trouble and had to clean his entire house. Up to that point he had no proof that you had stolen the chicken, and Mama was working on calming him down and making him think it had run away on its own. She had already sent Finny out to grab the chicken and take it back to the pen while they argued, but you wouldn't listen to me and got yourself in serious trouble. At that point Mama *had* to punish you and so you spent nearly three days cleaning his nasty hut."

Ynya shivered, remembering how much work that place was to muck out properly.

"He needed a wife."

"He *had* a wife, she lived in the hut next door. She had gotten so sick of him never cleaning anything, she built her own place to live."

"Well, why didn't you tell me to stop?"

"I did!" Synol did the motion again. "I was telling you to stop without words!"

Realization dawned on Ynya. She felt like an idiot as she remembered so many instances in her life when she had been clued in by a family member as to how to act, but had totally ignored them and done her own thing.

And nearly every one of those had gotten her into trouble, mostly by mouthing off to someone.

"I'm done."

Both girls whirled to face Finny. She stood in the doorway, dried tears streaked down her cheeks.

Chapter Fourteen

Ynya embraced her younger sister a split second before Synol wrapped them both in a powerful hug.

Ynya looked into the room, where she could just see the shadow of the creature in the cage. Something about his eyes told her there was still a frightening intelligence there.

A shudder ran down her spine as she watched him. He stood on hind legs, grasping the bars with his taloned hands and watching the three girls embrace.

There was still something familiar about him that Ynya still couldn't place. It was like she had seen his face before. *That can't be right.* She had never seen him in her entire life. Still, Ynya couldn't stop watching him.

He stared back, still raised up on two hind legs.

Like a human.

The thought sent a shiver down Ynya's spine. *He* had *been human at some point, just like Finny, hadn't he?*

For the first time, Ynya looked past the blackened, hairless skin and the gaunt features to see that there was a person in there. *Sure, he was twisted beyond recognition, but wasn't that the entire point of Reyoarfjell?*

The Queen's concentration camp had been designed to take normal people and turn them into something they were not. Soldiers were just one transition, but Skarmyord was another. This was just the next evolution, changing not only the mind, but the body as well.

Ynya had been awake too many nights, watching her sister Finny in that bizarre bestial form of hers loping around the snow, hunting rabbits and other small prey. Despite the depravity of seeing her sister change forms, Finny tended to act like two different beings; one human, one not.

Ynya forced the line of thought out of her head. She was venturing down another dark path from where she doubted there would be any reconciliation.

Finny needed to work things out for herself, and while she had Ynya and Synol to help her when she was in her normal, girl form, Finny needed more than they could give her.

Finny needed someone else...like him. Someone who went through the same things she did and survived.

Ynya pulled back to hold Finny at arm's length. Was she a little bit smaller than she had been?

"Finny, were you able to communicate with him? I heard the chirps and other sounds you two were making in there."

Finny nodded. "He's in a lot of pain, so I taught him some things Mama told us to calm our minds."

Ynya smiled. It was amazing how many skills their mother had taught them while growing up. So many of those lessons ended up being useful for them now. From focusing their minds, to proper use of their powers, to–

Ynya's mind went stark white as realization hit her.

Another, much larger shiver gripped her spine and yanked

her to a new reality. The chill ran down her arms and into her hands, making them twitch with anticipation.

Ynya broke away from her sisters' embrace and turned toward the creature in the cage.

"God's Below and Above."

"What's wrong?"

"Mama taught us a lot of things, right? Like how to focus our minds, and how to both hide and use our magic properly. She taught us hand signals, and the importance of family. Remember those stories she told about growing up and the games she used to play as a young one?"

Synol and Finny nodded.

"In all of her stories, she never once mentioned siblings, but she talked about friends. She talked about helping those friends accomplish things, and one of those was helping them escape from a prison, remember those stories?"

Synol's face took on a stricken look. "What are you getting at?"

"What if that prison she talked about was Reyoarfjell? What if her friends were her siblings? What if she wasn't able to get them all out or they died in the process and that was why she never talked about them to us? I never told you this, but I poured over the checkin books the Warden kept in his desk, and there were four Obliques logged in, each about a week apart. Nora and Mama came in a week after two other names. Mama didn't have just one sibling, she had three, just like us.

Ynya whirled around. "Think about it. If she had said we had an uncle or aunt we would have wanted to meet them, or at least ask questions about them that she wasn't prepared to answer.

"I think Mama knew what was going to happen to us and prepared us all to escape from the Frost Queen. I think she somehow knew the future and predicted what was going to happen, so she made sure to teach us how to do all these things to survive."

Tears streamed down Synol's stricken face; even Finny's was softened.

Ynya pursed her lips. "In fact, I think I know what Mama's magic was and how she knew what was going to happen."

Behind them, Captain Nora cleared her throat. "I'm sure Her Majesty will be happy to hear about that, since I was never able to figure it out myself."

Chapter Fifteen

C aptain Nora held Ynya's head to the stone floor as the Frost Queen paced in front of them.

Clack, clack, clack!

Every step of the shoes drove home just how much the Queen dominated the room. She was a woman who commanded respect. From her casual but deadly demeanor, to the skin-tight dresses she wore, to the intense magical aura she exhumed, to her metal-lined shoes, the Queen made sure everyone knew where she was and just how powerful she was.

Clack, clack, clack!

It was incredibly unnerving, the Queen walking just inches from Ynya's prone body.

Nora had dragged her up many flights of stairs to the top of the Frost Queen's castle. The room looked like a workshop, with a desk and chairs and half a dozen bookcases along the walls.

The stone in the Queen's study was impeccably maintained, except for the face print where Nora held Ynya to the polished marble.

Seconds ticked by, and the Queen continued to pace.

Ynya spoke, though it was difficult to do so given her position.

"I can't tell you because I am not entirely sure myself."

The Queen stopped pacing.

"Is that so? I have ways to make you talk, you know. Oh, let her up Nora, she's not going to do anything. You act like she could possibly harm me."

Ynya was surprised that the Frost Queen hadn't taken her magic again. Most likely it was a conscious choice to make sure Ynya understood just how insignificant the Queen thought she was. Yet again, the Queen wore her power on her sleeve in such a way that would almost seem disingenuous if she wasn't actually powerful enough to do it properly.

Luckily, Ynya hadn't told anyone but Synol and Finny about her mother's powers residing inside her. The only other people who might know had been the testers from Reyoarfjell, and she didn't know if they had managed to get their testing information results out to the Queen or not.

Hopefully not, given how soon after her testing the place was destroyed by Finny's wind magic.

Ynya stood, shoving Nora when she tried to grab Ynya's upper arm.

Ynya glanced back to her sisters in the doorway. Synol gave her the sign to keep her mouth shut, and Ynya replied with the sign that she understood.

One corner of the room held a raised stone dais with a large inscribed rune chiseled into the aged rock. Ynya wasn't sure of the rune's purpose, but she sensed an immense amount of power undulating within it.

The main focus of the room was the massive windowed

openings looking out over the frozen plains and the army encampment.

It was mid-day at this point, and the overhead sun diffused through the light snowfall, giving the whole scene a serene, calm ardor. The wind had died down a fair amount and Ynya could almost enjoy the serenity if it wasn't for the distant screams of the people on the spikes outside.

It was the same people she had seen from the ground. Back then she hadn't been close enough to hear them, but here, level with them, that's about all she heard.

It was an odd reality that she wanted the constant howl of the wind back. Then again, she was standing in front of the woman who had ordered her sisters kidnapped thus resulting in her parents' death. The whole world was an odd reality when you were on a quest to rescue your sisters from fates worse than death.

Finally standing, Ynya continued. "What does it matter, anyway? Your soldiers raped and killed my mother, so there isn't anything to be gained by knowing what magic she had."

Nora growled.

Captain Nora wore the same look on her face back in the Holmslatr prison. It was an expression that, at the time, Ynya had wondered about, but brushed off as a Captain irritated that her soldiers weren't following orders.

But now, knowing that Nora was her aunt, Ynya thought she understood better what the Captain had gone through at that moment.

It was one thing to follow orders from the Queen and kidnap your nieces, but it was another thing entirely to know that your sister was now dead because of those soldiers' uncontrolled lust.

The Frost Queen paced to a bookshelf and grabbed a thick

leather-bound tome in her arms. "I need to know because her powers might have been passed down to one of you, and knowing what she had initially will help me answer some questions."

"What questions?"

The Queen dropped the book on her desk and tugged at a ribbon in the middle.

"This book maps out the cycles of the moon, the stars, and the earth in relation to each other. This book covers about five thousand years of historical and future data, and as you can see, we are only halfway through the book. That means it will continue being useful for another two-thousand years."

The Queen planted a fingernail on the page, about halfway down one of the columns of data.

"Eight years ago, I opened this book and looked at what it told me. I did the same thing twelve years ago, and sixteen, and I want you to take a wild guess when the other time I consulted this book was."

Ynya swallowed, her throat suddenly dry. She glanced back to her sisters, all three standing in the doorway with the same terrified expression.

"Eighteen?"

The Frost Queen slammed the book closed. "Exactly! Now you can imagine just how curious I was when the stars told me about all four of your births, but the more interesting thing is that this doesn't just tell me when you were born, it also told me the details under which each of you were conceived."

The Queen put the book back on the shelf, then walked to the rune on the stone.

The Queen looked like she would step onto the rune, but stopped short, her face betraying her inability to proceed.

Interesting, so the rune didn't allow her on?

The Queen turned, folding her arms across her chest.

"This involved some further investigation, of course. This rune allows me to see through the Void. It was the only way I could find out the details I needed. Your mother managed to get pregnant with each of you at the correct time in order to produce a daughter."

She walked closer to Ynya. "She was so precise with her copulations that she managed to ensure not only your gender but seed a specific type of magic within you. In doing so, she ensured each of you had some other traits passed on, like the propensity to inherit or pass on your family's bloodline of magic, which I'm still trying to decipher.

"If that wasn't enough, she managed to birth you at just the right times to ensure you were born with all the traits she sought. She even went so far as keeping one of you in her womb for longer than any woman I've ever seen just to ensure you were born at the right time. Had she deviated by even one day then all the preparations might have been for naught. Yet she persevered. I dare say she impresses me to this day with her gumption and precise planning. Tis a shame she's not alive to serve me."

The Frost Queen stopped right in front of Ynya, squaring off to her.

"I know we women can sometimes get a little crazy when it comes to our offspring, but have you ever heard of a woman putting so much thought and care into when her children were conceived *and* born that she would go through an eleven month pregnancy just to ensure their child received a specific type of magic?"

The Queen stared at Finny for a long time before breaking her gaze back to Ynya.

Ynya heard Finny's feet shuffle across the floor.

Ynya wanted to squirm or run herself, but she knew she needed to stand against this tyrannical woman no matter how much it unnerved her.

"Tell me, Ynya Oblique, daughter of Talia Oblique, how did your mother manage to time all of these copulations and births so perfectly? The book I have is one of a kind, I stole it from my father before he imprisoned me here in the frozen north. It doesn't exist anywhere else, so how would your mother understand things that have never been seen by other human eyes?"

Chapter Sixteen

Y nya swallowed, trying to keep her nerves in check. "I don't exactly know. My mother never told any of us what her true magic was. We all had our own suspicions, but even as a young girl I asked her repeatedly what magic she had, and she would always find a way to change the subject."

"And what did you think she had?"

Talia Oblique's magic had been on Ynya's mind a lot lately, especially since she arrived here at the Queen's castle, but she wasn't about to tell any of that to Her Majesty.

Instead, while being dragged up some seven flights of stairs by her evil aunt, Ynya came up with the most probable explanation based on the outward evidence. It was a story she would insist on.

"When I was younger, I thought Mama could grow garden plants, but turns out that was just Synol with her earth magic. Then, I wondered if she could control the weather, but seems that had gone to Finny with her wind magic. But leaving those to the side, my best guess now is that Mama was able to predict the future."

"How so?" The Queen turned her back and strode toward the open window overlooking the falling snow.

"When Papa went on fishing trips, she would sometimes tell him to wait a day or two. Whenever she did that, despite the skies looking clear at the time, a storm came out of nowhere a couple days later. She had to have saved his life at least a dozen times over the years because she knew when storms were coming."

"Do you think she could control the weather?"

Ynya glanced back to her sisters again.

"No, just predict it."

The Queen nodded her head. "So your best guess, with all your observations, is that she had predictive magic? Do you have any other evidence for this theory of yours?"

"I think so. She also predicted crop failures and other things around town that allowed people to finish getting animals indoors before a big freeze came."

Ynya smirked. "She also sent me away on a fishing trip right before your troops showed up. I didn't realize it at the time, but she insisted I leave on my trip that day, thus ensuring I wasn't there when your soldiers arrived. So you tell me, Your Majesty, did your soldiers leak their plans, or could she predict the future?"

The whole conversation whirled around in Ynya's head. As much as she was trying to convince the Queen that Talia had predictive powers, internally, she was trying to decipher exactly what her mother actually had. Her mother had spent her entire life preparing her girls for this encounter. She had laid in the frozen snow for two days waiting for her daughter to come back from a fishing trip in order to gift her magic to Ynya. Ynya needed to learn what it was so she could properly use it to help them escape.

The Frost Queen paced back and forth in front of the window, her brows furrowed in thought.

Ynya chanced a look back at Synol, who held Finny with one hand and Meki with the other. Synol's mouth was drawn to her familiar unreadable line.

"And what do you think about these things, Captain Nora?"

Ynya glanced to the Skarmyord standing two paces away.

The woman in black frowned. "She never told me about any type of magic she had, but that doesn't mean she didn't have any. My own magic wasn't unlocked until my Enlightenments, it's possible that whatever she had wasn't unlocked until then. Did the records from Reyoarfjell not state their findings on her?"

The Queen shook her head. "Those particular ones, along with a handful of other specific ones, were found to be missing when I looked for them upon discovery of the girl's births. You wouldn't know anything about that would you, Ynya?"

Ynya shrugged. "I didn't even know there were records kept. We destroyed the entire camp once we got the prisoners out safely, so I can't tell you much there. Perhaps if you find the remains of the Warden you can piece him back together and reanimate him to find the answers you seek."

The Queen pursed her lips and furrowed her brow, her long fingernail still tapping the desk in front of her. "You think you are so clever, don't you, Ynya? Well, the world is much grander than you could possibly know, and I have been around a long time."

She turned back to Nora. "Your sister escaped the camp?"

Nora nodded. "Yes, Your Majesty."

"I remember when that happened. That was one of your

first failures under my service. I punished you extensively for that if I recall." A small smile spread across the Queen's lips.

Ynya shuddered.

Nora's already white face paled, but her expression did not betray her thoughts. "You did, Your Majesty."

Ynya wasn't sure how effective the Queen's threats were to a Skarmyord. The Enlightenments didn't seem to change the personalities of the soldiers near as much as the Queen would probably have liked, so it was possible that the Skarmyord still retained more of their humanity than the Queen wanted.

That might be why she had to constantly exude magic and power, to keep everyone just fearful enough that they wouldn't dare betray her.

Ynya had spent what time she could today watching the pattern of the guards, and the various nearly-hidden doors that the kitchen staff used. She counted the steps leading up to the Queen's room, and now she watched her long-lost aunt's facial expressions, looking for any sign of humanity.

The Frost Queen tapped her long fingernail on the wood desk. "So what we have here is a mysterious family of mages, all female, that have come up through the ranks. One has served me all these years, while another has gone and done something so amazing, I have to wonder which one ultimately served me the best."

Nora gulped.

Ynya tensed. It was suddenly very cold, and the Frost Queen pulled an immense amount of magic to her.

But...it wasn't just the Frost Queen, most of the snap in the air came from...behind Ynya.

From Meki?

Ynya turned and looked at her sister. The young girl's eyes were glazed over and unfocused, like she was in a trance.

Turning allowed Ynya to get a feel for the power difference between her sister and the Frost Queen's magic.

It was immediately noticeable to Ynya, that the flow of power went from Meki to the Queen, then out into the room, but the interesting part was that Meki's well of magic felt deeper and broader than the Queen's. While the Queen's magic swirled around in the room in a blizzard, the true power of Meki's frost magic wasn't being tapped, while the Queen's was.

Is Meki stronger than the Queen?

The magic around the Queen swelled, filling the expansive room A howling wind whipped at their skirts. Icy frost clung to their hair, weighing it down as it tried to fly away with each gust.

The Queen finally relented. The magic dissipated, and the room returned to the calm it once contained.

Only now most everything contained a small layer of ice across its surface.

The Queen looked at Nora, then Ynya. "I don't know what your mother hid from me, but I should be grateful that she did. Her gift of you four girls turned out to be a blessing of the Gods, and I have plans for each of you. Especially you, Finny."

Finny's eyes widened at the Queen's response.

Ynya turned to look at her sister, but upon meeting her gaze, Finny pursed her lips and turned her head to look out the window.

What was that all about? Ynya asked herself.

The Queen took a step out from behind her desk. "Each of you is going to serve me in unique ways, but I want to start with you, Ynya. The rest of you have other places to be, and I'll have Nora here escort you where you are supposed to go. But Ynya and Meki are coming with me."

"What are we doing?" Ynya asked.

The Queen smirked but continued walking toward the door.

Ynya glanced between her sisters, even searching the face of Captain Nora, but no one let on what the Queen meant.

Finally, passing by Ynya and following the Queen, Meki sighed. "We're going to spar, dummy. It's what we do here, to focus and improve our magic."

Chapter Seventeen

"Again until you win!" The Queen barked.

Ynya thought she was going to die. The Queen had her battling Meki for the last two hours. Her arms ached, her head pounded, and her side still healed from an ice spike that had cut into her an hour earlier.

Two earth mages stepped forward to repair the arena like they had done nearly a dozen times before.

Ynya eyed Meki, who sat down to meditate as soon as the match ended.

This whole situation was surreal. Her youngest sister was so much better than her. *And I didn't even know about Meki's powers until this morning!*

Ynya growled under her breath. This last match had at least lasted nearly three minutes, but that was only because Ynya ran and hid for a while, trying to draw Meki out.

What is she trying to do to me?

The Queen sat on a throne of ice near the exit to the expansive training room. A soldier carrying a scroll stood a few paces away, trying to get the Queen's attention without inter-rupting her. He'd been there for nearly an hour.

Just speak to the poor guy already.

Even if Ynya wasn't gaining any ground on her abilities, she tried to use the opportunity to learn little bits of informa-tion about the Queen.

People stood for hours waiting for her to acknowledge them.

She also had one hell of a temper on her. Twice she'd done the same frost rage thing she had done earlier in her office.

Despite their vast differences, Ynya understood the rage boiling just under the surface. It was a trait they both shared, much to Ynya's chagrin.

Still, it surprised Ynya that she seemed to have better control over her emotions than a powerful Queen who had lived at least a couple hundred years so far.

I wonder how old is she, anyway?

Ynya had been through enough in her short life to realize that sometimes, not expressing that anger outwardly was the right thing to do.

Despite the power difference between the two, the Queen, in a lot of ways, acted like a petulant child. Because she never had anyone more powerful than she was smack her down a time or two, she had nowhere to go to learn lessons of life.

Like when your eight-year-old sister beats you so soundly and so quickly you're left bewildered how she managed to do such a thing.

Ynya grit her teeth.

Running away didn't work. Meki beat her every time when it came to ranged combat.

One would think that a matchup between a fire and a frost mage would be exciting, and if Ynya could launch her fire through the air, she supposed it would be, but Ynya's inability to shoot fire and Meki's propensity towards ice spikes meant Ynya was constantly on the run.

So stop running, you stupid girl.

Was it that simple? Maybe it was time to try something drastic. As far as she knew, the Queen wouldn't allow her to do anything else until she won.

"Again!" The Queen's snappy voice cut through the air.

Meki opened her eyes, still sitting in the same meditative position.

Ynya ran around a pillar, hoping to draw Meki in like last time. Two spikes slammed into the ground just to her side. She darted left, her shoulder brushing against the large stone pillar. Another spike slammed into the ground just in front of her.

How is she seeing me around the pillar?

They were under instruction to *try* to avoid harming one another, which Ynya was happy to follow, but Meki apparently didn't know what that meant, or had been given overriding directives.

Ynya couldn't be entirely sure, as she hadn't been given much of a chance to properly speak with her younger sister. She needed to know why Meki so willingly did these actions for the Queen. Had she been tricked, or did she genuinely believe the Queen was her mother? Perhaps the Queen had cast a spell on the poor girl to manipulate her memory, or force her to say those things.

Perhaps it was all a cruel joke put on by the Queen to make her feel more important than anyone else.

Either way, Ynya needed some alone time with her sister.

Three more spikes slammed down. Two in front of her, and one to the right. She dodged left, just as three more came down in front of her.

Pillar to her left, three spikes in front, one to the right, she turned.

Slam!

And just like that, she was trapped.

Dammit!

"Again!"

Three tries later, Ynya decided sneaking was no good. She also surmised that Meki used the light dusting of snow over the entire room to track her.

It was the only thing that could possibly allow her to sense Ynya from the other side of the pillar, unless Meki had some other unknown ability in that regard.

Ynya couldn't keep doing this all day long. It was time to start trying new things and hope she made progress.

This time, when the Queen yelled for the match to start, Ynya ran, but instead of running away from Meki, she ran toward her.

Straight toward her.

Meki froze for a full second at the sudden change in tactic, and that was all the time Ynya needed to close significant distance between the two.

By the time Meki had recovered and cast her first spell, Ynya was only a few feet away.

Spikes slammed down into the ground, but Ynya bent down and rammed into them with her shoulder.

The ice shattered into thousands of pieces, spraying Ynya's face with dust, but she continued to pump her legs directly at her little sister.

Meki must have expected her to dodge sideways because more spikes slammed down into the ground behind and to the left of Ynya.

Too little, too late.

Ynya jumped, reaching out and grabbing onto her sister at full-speed. She realized her size and weight could have caused serious harm to the little girl, but she was beyond caring at this point. The Queen would have probably yelled at her for slowing down anyway. This wasn't a game of tag, it was a true fight with stakes that would leave at least one of them trapped or injured.

As she sailed through the air, Ynya pushed heat into her extremities. She wrapped her arms and legs around her sister and held on for dear life.

The sooner she satisfied whatever twisted outcome the Queen wanted, the sooner she could move on from this.

Both girls fell to the floor, but as Ynya held on tightly, she whispered in Meki's ear.

"Our Mama was killed by the Queen, and I am here to take you back to your family."

Chapter Eighteen

"And why did you think you won the last three times as opposed to the first dozen or so?"

Ynya stood straight and tall. "I used the element of surprise to my advantage."

"Yes, but why did it work three times in a row?"

Ynya looked over at Meki, who's eyes were wide with a mixture of confusion and worry. Each time Ynya managed to get in close to Meki, she had continued to tell her things that she needed to hear. Ynya supposed that the shocked Meki was simply distracted by the things Ynya told her, so that she hadn't been able to concentrate properly on the matches.

Either way, it was accomplishing two things; Ynya was winning, which seemed to please the Queen, and she and Meki were finally able to communicate in private.

Even though it was a one-way conversation.

Still, Ynya had a lot to say to her long-lost sister.

She told Meki that Synol's husband had been a tyrant and Synol had killed him for his abuse. She told her that Finny had been with Meki the whole trip after their capture, but they got separated when they got to Reyoarfjell, as well as telling her that Finny has been seriously abused and changed permanently because of all the hurtful practices of the Frost Queen.

Each one rattled Meki more than Ynya expected. While she felt bad that he had to tell these horrible things to her youngest sister, she found it effective in pulling her away from the Queen's sinister clutches.

Sometimes, the hard truth is the best truth.

She'd lucked out with her decision to tackle and talk rather than hide and lose.

She replied to the Queen. "Each time I varied the method for getting in close. Since I do not have the ability to use fire from range, I must get in close in order to apply heat directly to the target."

Ynya looked at Meki once again. "Your Majesty." It still churned her stomach to even talk to the woman who had killed her parents, but she was in the den of the bear, and she had to tread lightly in order to escape. "Meki seems a little rattled, and I would like to try out this meditation stuff she's been doing between matches. Do you mind if she and I meditate?"

Ynya waved her hand at the soldier who had been standing for well over an hour at this point. "You could address this man's scroll or something."

The Queen turned her head, acting like she had just noticed the young man for the first time. "Oh, well, yes. Soldier, what news have you?"

Ynya walked to Meki and took her hand to lead her away.

Meki pulled her hand away. "I will not hold your hand. You are the enemy." Her voice wasn't loud, but it wasn't soft either. Luckily the Queen was focused on the scroll the soldier had handed her.

Ynya lowered her voice and spoke to Meki. "The Queen said we were to meditate, so we're going to do that."

She grabbed Meki's hand again and took her a dozen more feet away before sitting down.

Meki closed her eyes and placed both hands together.

Ynya followed suit.

"Meki, I know the Queen has poisoned you against me, but I'm not here to do you any harm. I wasn't lying about all the things we've gone through trying to get to you. Synol killed her husband, Finny's been tortured, I've been stabbed and had my magic taken away more times than I can count. We did it all to come get you. We are here to rescue you from the Queen and take you back home."

Meki ignored her.

To the side, the Queen threw down the scroll. "Gods Below!"

The Queen's rage peaked and blasted the area around her with a gust of frigid wind.

Icy cold rain pelted Ynya, but she turned her heat up to counteract the cold. Inside her skin, she was safe and warm, and despite being this close to the Queen's temper tantrum once again, she was the closest she'd been to her sister for more than a few moments since this whole mess started. She didn't know how they were going to escape, but she was making progress.

It's just a matter of time.

Meki whimpered.

The Queen continued her tirade. Each time the Queen swore or pushed frost magic into the room, Meki flinched.

Each time, Ynya felt Meki's magic surge from her to the Queen.

Ynya scooted closer to her youngest sister. She was so small and fragile. Her once-rosy cheeks had lost some of their color, and her bright red curly hair was covered in a slight dusting of frost. Despite her innate frost magic, Meki shivered.

Ynya wasn't sure if it was from the cold or from the connection the Frost Queen had to her magic. Either way, Ynya was here to comfort her baby sister.

Ynya grabbed Meki's hands and poured a moderate amount of heat into the girl. Meki didn't pull away this time. In fact, she met Ynya's eyes, a pained expression on her face.

"I can't believe the incompetence going on in the front lines!" The Queen was on her feet, screaming at the young man. "We are on a timeline here, and we cannot deviate from this no matter what! The window for this is incredibly tight and we cannot afford any delays!"

The Queen stomped again, sending out another wave of frost.

Meki flinched.

Ynya squeezed harder. "It's okay, little sister. I'll find a way to ensure the Queen can't hurt you anymore."

The Queen finished, jotting something down on the back of the scroll and handed it back to the solider, who quivered a few feet away. His face was turning blue from the frost, but he hadn't moved from his spot the entire time.

"Get back to the Feond and tell my army that any delays will be dealt with swiftly and painfully. If I have to wait for the next Transference, I will personally torture every soul for the duration!"

Ynya dropped Meki's hands after giving her another squeeze and scooted a few inches away.

She wanted to make sure the Queen's wrath didn't transfer to her, or worse, Meki.

Meki was scared. That was clear, but she also was brainwashed into thinking that her sisters were her enemy.

At least Ynya knew what the problems were, and understanding your enemy turned out to be quite helpful.

"Enough meditating, let's go again!"

Meki and Ynya stood in unison.

Chapter Nineteen

The four sisters had been left to eat by themselves, strangely enough, without Captain Nora, their constant shadow. Even Meki had been left behind while the Queen and Nora were away "dealing with business."

Ynya figured it was just a ruse for Nora to tell the Queen everything they had been doing.

Ynya used the opportunity to do the same thing with Synol. She also wanted to know what Synol and Finny did while she and Meki sparred. She started with what the Queen had said to the soldier.

"What do you think she's working on?" Synol asked in a hushed tone.

Ynya shrugged. "I'm not sure. I've heard the term Feond a couple times now, but I'm not entirely sure what it means. Have you ever heard that term?"

Synol shook her head. "Sorry, I don't know what it means."

Ynya indicated Finny. "And how are things going with her?"

Finny hadn't eaten much, instead she had watched Meki

with a somber expression for five minutes before moving a few seats closer to her younger sister.

Synol frowned. "She spent more time with that...creature again. She even has a name for him."

"Let me guess, Firtze?"

Synol's eyes scrunched in confusion. "Actually, she calls him Pain, but that name sounds familiar. How did you know that?"

Ynya's heart ached at the memory. "Firtze was one of the mages who was trapped in the caravan. He helped me escape that one time before I came back for you. He helped Joanne and Tyrain survive before they were captured and taken to Reyoarfjell. He was with the Translator before Finny."

Synol sucked in air, a stark expression on her face. "God's Below. That was all before we got there?"

Ynya nodded, suddenly not hungry. "I didn't put it all together until I saw him down in there, but he looked at me with familiar human-like eyes. I remembered what Joanne had told me and realized that he was the one they said had been carted off by Nora back here, to this castle. Finny might call him Pain because I think that part of his soul died to create the monster. He might have been called Firtze before, but Pain is just as good a name I suppose. It's probably more accurate than Firtze."

Ynya shuddered as a thought came to her. "I hope that's not how Finny thinks of herself."

Ynya grabbed a roll and stuffed it into her pocket. She wasn't sure why it felt so good to have a roll on her, but it did. Maybe it was the two months of living in the cold and sleeping on the ground that had gotten to her, but knowing she had another meal available in the future helped ease her worry now.

She glanced down the table at the two girls.

"What is it?"

Synol's voice was strained as she tried to keep herself from bursting into tears. "I've seen her change to that beast before."

Finny generally changed out of view of the camp, but a few times Ynya had been awake for it. She hadn't known that Synol had seen it. "I thought you were asleep?"

Synol tucked a lock of Ynya's hair behind her ear. "Sweet Ynya. I know you haven't slept much these last few weeks. I don't know what's keeping you up at night, but you not sleeping means I wasn't able to sleep myself."

The terror that had gripped Ynya's heart relaxed, replaced with a warm love toward her sister. "Don't worry about me, let's just get the girls out of here safely. That said, I'm curious what the Queen is planning. She indicated there wasn't much time until she arrived at whatever this Feond is, which troubles me. Maybe whatever she's working on will keep her distracted enough that we can find a way to escape."

Synol nodded. "Let's just take it one day at a time, then. We can't exactly walk out the front door, so playing it safe is probably the better option. If she takes us to the Feond, then we might be able to slip away in the chaos of traveling, just like you and I did last time."

Ynya frowned. "I don't know that it will be easier this time. I'm sure they will chain me like they did last time, and not make the same mistake again. In fact, I'm surprised the Queen allows me to keep my magic."

"It's because she isn't afraid of us."

Ynya nodded. "I figured. She's foolish, but I can't complain too much. It's nice not being so cold all the time. As long as we don't rock the boat and follow all her directions, I think we're in the clear. We just need to figure out what the Feond is, and where, so we can figure out how to escape."

Finny spoke up. "The Feond is a spell that seals the Queen away in the Frozen North."

The older sisters exchanged a look before glancing down the table at their younger sister.

"How do you know this?"

Finny frowned. "She told me. She told me that Pain and I will be an integral part of the plan."

"She told you her plan?" Synol stood.

Finny shook her head, her eyes not leaving Meki. "All I know is that Pain and I will be part of it, as will you two, and Meki here."

Meki's eyes flinched at her name, but she focused on the food before her.

Ynya strode over to Meki's chair and knelt down. "Meki, dear sister. Do you know anything about what the Queen is planning?"

An icy voice from behind them filled the room. "Why don't you just ask me yourself?"

Chapter Twenty

Ynya turned.

The Frost Queen stood a few paces into the doorway, with Captain Nora by her side. Both women held themselves with poise and forbearance, each bearing their own brand of condescension gracing their faces.

"Well, come. Sit and eat with me. I assume you have a lot of questions."

The Queen took three steps forward and sat in her chair at the head of the table.

Ynya glanced at Synol, who grimaced and raised her eyebrows.

Ynya took her seat next to the Queen, followed by the rest of the girls.

The Queen picked up a chicken leg and narrowed her eyes at it. "I see you've spent most of your time talking rather than eating, but I suppose that is to be expected. Go on, if you have questions, ask them. Nora here will be happy to answer the easy ones while I eat. I daresay I am quite famished."

She bit into the chicken. Juices from the meat squished, splashing the table.

"What is the Feond?" Ynya finally managed to get out, the meat juices distracting her.

Captain Nora took a step forward. "The Feond is a barrier created by the Queen's father to trap her in the frozen north."

Ynya glanced at Finny, whose somber expression hadn't seemed to change at all with the Queen's presence.

Synol spoke up, her face exhibiting a curiosity Ynya hadn't seen in a while. "So there is a King?"

The Frost Queen stood and screamed. Icy frost pummeled everyone at the table.

Meki screamed as well, but it wasn't a rage-filled scream like the Queen, it was the scream of a young girl being hurt for her magic.

Ynya felt the flow between the two, she could almost see it through the mist emanating from the Queen.

Ynya's heart slowed, as she took in the scene. She watched everyone's expressions go from nervousness to terror.

Then, it was over. The Queen panted, her hands on the table before her. She spoke with a biting anger. "He is no king of mine. He is nothing but a traitor to his race. He locked me away up here when my brother and I rebelled against him and his traitorous ways. My brother died saving my life. I have been left all alone up here, trying to figure out a way to get across the barrier."

Ynya ventured another question. "How does that involve us?"

The Queen stared at Ynya for a long time before answering. "Your magic will help me take down the Feond."

"How are we going to use our magic to help you?"

"I will give instructions once I need your help, but for now you don't need to worry about that portion."

Synol spoke up, brushing some frost off her forearms. "What about after that? Are you going to let us go after we help you take down the Feond?"

The Queen picked back up her chicken leg, looked at it a second, then threw it down on the table and grabbed her wine goblet. She took a sip, her eyes closed as she drained the liquid.

She slammed the goblet down on the table and looked back at Synol. "I don't care what you do. You can do whatever you want."

"Wait." Ynya started to stand but caught herself. She didn't want to seem like she was threatening the Queen. "Once we help you through the barrier, you will allow us, all four of us, to go home?"

The Queen looked to Nora for a second before turning back to the table. "I am not an unreasonable woman. I have my needs, like anyone else, and once those have been met, I have no reason to keep you here. So yes. Once you four have helped me across the barrier, then I will release you from my servitude. You can do whatever you wish after that. Go back to your little fishing village for all I care, for the North will not be of my concern anymore."

Ynya's chest swelled with hope and joy. She looked at her three sisters in turn. Synol's hopeful eyes seemed to match her joy. Meki looked pained, but hopeful. Finny, as usual, didn't seem to share in any expressions of joy any longer.

Still, this was great news.

"When do we leave?" Synol asked.

"Leave?"

Yes, don't we need to travel to this location? The Feond?"

The Queen shook her head. "Oh, no. You won't need to

worry about that. All the work is to take place here, at my castle. Everything I need is here, or will be here very soon. In the meantime, I will train your magic to increase your capacity for casting, and you can enjoy the time until you are called upon to help me.

Chapter Twenty-One

After dinner, the four girls were shown to a room one floor down from the Queen's study.

Captain Nora stood in the doorway, a stern look on her face. "I will be outside here all night. You are not allowed to leave."

"That's fine," Ynya replied. "I'm looking forward to a good night's sleep anyway."

Nora eyed her for a long time, her eyebrows twitching. She then looked to Synol and frowned before closing the door.

Synol replied by mimicking the same glare that been on Nora's face, then she chuckled. Ynya couldn't help herself and finally joined Synol in laughing at the ridiculous look the Skarmyord wore.

Even Meki grimaced, which was an improvement.

We're finally together and alone!

Ynya felt so relieved.

Ynya eyed a couple of the tapestries and a large mirror on one of the walls. Most likely one or two of those were listening spots for the Queen's henchmen, but at least they didn't have a babysitter follow them into their actual bed.

More importantly, they were finally together.

Ynya basked in the knowledge that, regardless of the trials and pain they had gone through, things were looking up for them.

"The Queen is not telling the truth." Finny said.

All the elation Ynya experienced deflated in an instant as Finny's matter-of-fact statement brought it all crashing down to reality.

Ynya closed her eyes to center herself. Part of her wanted to snap at her sister for ruining the mood of the room, but Finny was probably the only one not being distracted by the moment and was staying vigilant. It wasn't fair or right of Ynya to snap at Finny in this situation.

"What do you mean?"

Finny frowned before sitting down on one of the chairs to the side. "I don't know, but there was something about her."

"Like her mood?"

Finny shook her head. "Her smell. Something was wrong with her smell. She was very careful with the words she used, but there was something big she didn't tell us."

"What do you think it could be?"

Finny shrugged. "I don't know, but something about the way she commands my magic chilled when she said she would release us. It was like she tightened her grip on my magic when she spoke."

Meki drew in a sharp breath. "I felt the same."

Synol embraced her youngest sister. "Meki, I know this is hard for you, but I want you to know that we are all here for you."

Meki stared blankly at her big sister, her lip trembling

below softened eyes. "She knows everything that happens in this castle."

Synol gave her a pained smile in return, tucking Meki's tight curls behind her right ear. "We know, sweetie. We have nothing to hide from her, even if she is listening to us right now, she doesn't scare us. We have gone through a lot to get here to see you, and nothing she does to us is going to take that away. We came here for you, not her."

Meki turned to Ynya. "What you told me earlier, about my Mama, about our home...that is all true?"

Ynya nodded. "Now that we are here, we are going to find a way to get you home. I know Mama and Papa aren't there anymore, but we are going to do whatever we can to try to put your life back together in Marsfjord."

Meki's face lit up at the mention of her hometown, but then she turned sad, and looked at the hallway door. "She says I have to go with her to Megean Fields."

"You don't have to do anything you don't want to," Synol replied. "We are here now and we will protect you. I know she controls your magic, just like she does Finny."

Meki shook her head. "She doesn't really control my magic, but she did link our magics together as soon as she helped me Bloom. Our magics are now linked and she can pull from my frost magic whenever she wants."

Synol glanced at Finny, then at Ynya. "That doesn't matter. She said that once she is done with us, we are free to go. I think all we have to do is wait and help her with her spell, then we can go home."

Ynya spoke up. "But what about the lying? What about her smell?"

Finny shook her head. "I could be wrong. Ever since I got here, I've been confused and not thinking straight. Pain calls to me constantly, wanting to be let out and trying to get me to change to be more like him."

Synol stared at Ynya, her eyes wide, then cocked her head toward Finny a couple times.

It took a second, but Ynya finally understood Synol's message.

Oh!

Ynya walked over to sit on the arm of the chair that Finny occupied.

"Finny, just like Synol told Meki, we are here for you, no matter what. You are our kin, you are our sister, and family is the most important thing. I don't care what they did to you, I only care that you are safe and loved. No matter what you look like or who you are now, you are still my sister and I love you unconditionally."

Finny looked up at Ynya, her mouth cocked to one side in an almost half-smile. It was probably the happiest Finny had looked in a long time. "Thank you. I just worry about Pain. He was the first experimented on back...there...and he has no one else. He must obey the Queen, like she is his leader."

Ynya thought about telling the girls about the three earrings she had in her pocket. *Maybe temporarily disconnecting Finny's magic would mean that the Queen couldn't control her?*

But Ynya only had one of the removable types, and one of the explosive types. If only she had retrieved more of the first type, they might have come in handy for them to escape. But at the time she'd been so pre-occupied with destroying them for the pain they'd caused countless individuals over the years, she hadn't thought that they might come in useful later on.

Once again, her short-sighted thinking had long-term consequences.

Ynya wished she knew exactly what the third golden type did. She hadn't gotten a straight answer out of the Warden before killing him.

She decided now wasn't the right time to bring up her secret. None of the others knew she had the earrings, and that meant the secret wouldn't be revealed to the Queen. It was probably best to keep it under wraps for now.

"Enough worry for tonight. I think we all should go to bed, and get a good night's sleep. We have time to spend together and be a family once again. As long as we are together, then nothing can stop us."

Chapter Twenty-Two

The next three days were a blur of activity, with the Queen keeping Ynya incredibly busy with early morning sparring sessions against all of her sisters. Every single time she sparred, she ran into the same issues she had from past sessions.

They were all faster than her.

They were all more powerful than her.

But most of all, they had ranged attacks that Ynya simply couldn't match.

Ynya finally had enough, and lay on her back, the cold seeping in through the white marble flooring of the indoor arena.

"Have you given up already?" The Frost Queen loomed over her, her right foot tapping an irritated rhythm on the stone beside Ynya's head. The pace doubled, but still matched the constant beat of the air and pulse of life that surrounded the Frost Queen's castle.

"I can't do it. Unless I can close the distance between any of them, I just can't do anything."

The Queen stopped tapping, a frown forming on her face.

All around them, Ynya felt magic swelling as the Queen's face turned in on itself, scrunching up tighter and tighter as rage overtook her normal stern look.

She was going to unleash on Ynya, and Ynya didn't rightly care right now. She was too tired and just wanted to rest.

Finny stepped forward, bowing to the Queen. "My Lady, perhaps it is time for a break? I can take Ynya down to meet Pain."

There was a hitch in the frost magic being pulled into the Queen, then, after an agonizing long wait, she released the magic, allowing it all to dissipate back into the Void.

The Queen was back to her normally stern, pointed face. She studied Finny for a long while before pursing her lips. "You grow closer. I see your affection for him. Do not fight it, for it will make things easier for you in the future."

The Queen raised her foot, holding it over Ynya's head.

Ynya flinched, thinking the Queen was going to kick her in the head, but she didn't move her whole body. There was no point fighting against the Queen. If she wanted to squash Ynya's head right now with her foot, she could.

Instead, the Queen pressed the cold sole of her shoe against Ynya's forehead. The frigid metal sapped her warmth faster than anything she'd ever experienced before, but released when the Queen retracted her foot.

"Go with your sister. See how obedience is earned around this place, then come back well-rested because I am growing tired of your inability to win against your sisters. I want you to think really hard about how you can possibly overtake them. My patience is thin and you have already been a massive thorn in my ass for long enough."

The Queen turned. "Synol and Meki! Time for training!"

Finny held out a hand, which Ynya stared at for a couple seconds before taking.

Her forehead hurt, despite the Queen not jabbing her with her foot, something about whatever she did left an indelible pain on her forehead. The cold spread through her skull and created a sharp throbbing ache.

She took Finny's hand and together, they walked toward the stairs that led down into the place with the animals.

By the time they arrived at the iron door, Ynya's head was down to a dull throb. She was also exhausted – from the early-morning activities, the lack of a breakfast, and pouring an immense amount of heat into her forehead to counteract the bizarre cold the Frost Queen had used on her.

What was all that for? Was she testing me?

Ynya didn't want to dwell too much on the rationale of a hyper-sensitive and tyrannical leader. She was pure evil, and whatever she did was symptomatic of her condition.

Worrying about the why-ifs and how-fors was simply a waste of time.

Time.

Something about that word resonated at an intimate level with Ynya.

Finny opened the door.

The cacophonous creak of the hinges filled the small hall-way, grating on Ynya's nerves, pulling her from her thoughts.

Then the smell hit her nostrils.

Ynya recoiled, a normal reaction to the situation of being in a dark, damp basement of a tyrannical overlord, and having a rusty iron door hurt your ears.

The smell was just adding to an already untenable situation.

But Ynya glanced at Finny, noting the look on her face.

Suddenly, all the problems in Ynya's life melted away. Her forehead, ears, and sinuses forgotten as she watched her younger sister don a face she hadn't seen in ages.

Peace.

How? What? Who?

Ynya looked into the room, through the bars of the cage, and to the frightening beast within, and it all made sense. Even the Queen noticed, and seemed to encourage it.

Finny was falling in love.

Or at least she had a friend that understood her unique past and trauma-filled changes.

Either one was fine by Ynya.

Ynya didn't move. She just stood there, watching her sister's bouncy gate as she padded across the room and to the bars.

Ynya knew that Finny had been lost, adrift like an abandoned fishing boat, caught by the tide. She'd been through far too much in a short time.

Ripped from her mother's arms, caged and tortured. She had been alone for so long, not knowing if any of her sisters were out there, trying to get to her.

Even Meki, forced to live with the Frost Queen, at least had someone who feigned to care for her.

But Finny had been through the most. Abandoned at every turn, then tortured by the Gods Below themselves.

Ynya couldn't take any of this small amount of joy away from her sister. She just couldn't.

A small smile graced Ynya's lips as she watched the interact through the bars.

Of all the places to smile, it had to be this. I'll take it.

Ynya let out a small prayer to the Gods Above to watch

over her small family, and even take care of Pain, for he was the primary joy in her sister's life.

From man to beast, he was the key to keeping Finny happy.

Ynya allowed her smile to broaden as she watched the two interact in their own odd way, and it was at that moment that she saw Firtze's eyes once again through the beast's milky gaze.

She *had* seen them before, she was sure of it.

Ynya was transported months before, a fiery spark between her and Firtze. His smile and his nod to her as she turned back to save Synol from the carriage.

At the time he had understood.

Ynya eyed the beast once more, a smile already on her lips.

She nodded back to the beast, who had caught her eye once again just like they had done so long ago in the snow.

Only this time it was Ynya's turn to nod her acceptance. She knew he was the best bet to save her sister, and Ynya was proud to welcome him into the family.

Chapter Twenty-Three

"Again!"

Ynya leaned against the pillar to take a quick breather while the Queen's mages repaired the arena. She glanced across the arena toward Synol, who hadn't broken a sweat.

The two eyed each other. Synol smiled.

Ynya frowned.

I think she's liking this, trouncing me before I can move.

And all before the sun was even warming the eastern sky.

Despite their agreement to not harm each other, the Queen had other plans for them, and promised torture unless she felt each girl was giving her best.

Synol was incredibly powerful, and Ynya got more and more frustrated with each match. Just like with Meki, Ynya couldn't get close enough to strike, and more often than not, the entire match was over as soon as it began due to Synol's ability to raise up pillars that trapped her.

Ynya had to admit that it was the easiest, most time-effective method of ending the match. But after six of those in a row, the Queen told Synol to come up with a new tactic.

The Queen wanted Ynya to fight. She didn't just want her defeated over and over or even tortured with magic. When Ynya wasn't able to counter a certain tactic, the Queen changed the rules to allow Ynya a way to stay competitive.

Despite her frustration with the exercises, Ynya's mind was on alert the entire time. She sought to understand the reasons behind the Queen's instructions.

Despite her tyrannical and erratic nature, the Queen seemed to want even fights between the girls. It was odd behavior for someone who lashed out at the slightest inference that she wasn't the most powerful being on the planet.

Ynya also found it curious that the Queen herself administrated these matches. The Queen had to be a very busy woman, right? After all, she was preparing to take down the barrier that separated her from her father in the south. She had rounded up her entire army to infiltrate the lands.

So why, in the midst of the most important thing in her life, was she officiating sparring matches between two sisters? Why didn't she get Nora to handle them?

And she wasn't just casually watching at the front either, she studied the girls carefully. She watched Synol cast spells and sometimes asked for clarification on why she chose that specific spell or method. She even grilled Ynya on why she didn't try something a certain way.

It was curious behavior, and that was why Ynya payed attention to it. The Queen wasn't just watching them for fun, and she certainly had important things to do, but she chose to be here.

"Ynya!"

"Yes, Your Majesty?"

"You have so much potential locked up inside of you, yet you barely use ten-percent of your power. Why is that?"

Ynya meted out her words carefully to avoid snapping at the Queen. "I can't close the distance between us. I can only use my heat when I can touch an object, so the only way I can defeat her is to get close."

The Queen pursed her lips, clearly thinking Ynya was lying to her. "Are you sure that is all you can do?"

Ynya was confused and her frustration came out in her reply. "You think I'm not trying? I'm doing everything I can to get to her."

The Queen frowned again, finally getting out of her seat and pacing in front of it. "I sense an incredible power within you, but you never seem to use it. I want to know why."

Even without a direct threat, Ynya felt like she had just been cornered. It reminded her of the time, years ago, when she had first come across the frost bear deep inside his lair.

This was a hundred times worse than that, and Ynya knew why.

The Queen knows I have my mother's magic!

She wanted to glance toward Synol, but she did everything she could to not betray her true thoughts. She stripped herself of emotion and focused on making the words come out as naturally as possible.

"I'm sorry, but I don't know what you're talking about."

The Queen frowned, but stopped pacing. "Very well, but know this. If you can't figure out how to use your magic soon, I might have to employ other methods to help you figure it out." She paused before sitting down in her chair. "Ynya, you think you aren't as powerful as your sisters, but you are wrong. You have an incredible magic locked inside your heart, and I'm going to whatever it takes to help you break it free."

***

"We're in big trouble, Synol."

Ynya paced in front of the door after Nora escorted them both back to their rooms to bathe and change for breakfast. Meki and Finny were already gone, so it was the perfect time to talk to Synol.

"Why? What's wrong?"

Ynya stopped, grabbing Synol by her arms and lowering her voice to a whisper. "She knows I have more magic than I am using, and if she figures out what it is, then she's going to do the same thing to me that she did to Meki and take it for herself."

Synol studied Ynya's face a bit before replying. "Do you know what the magic is?"

Ynya's stomach roiled.

In fact, she had spent some time over the last couple days mulling over what type of magic she had inside of her. The clues were there, little things happening to her since she left her hometown of Marsfjord stuck in her mind, like when she fought the woman in white and survived.

She hadn't survived by luck alone, something else had been at play.

She glanced around to make sure no one was watching them, then hugged Synol so she could whisper into her ear. "I think so, but I haven't been willing to test it fully until I was alone."

Synol hugged her back. "Then I will figure out a way for you to get some privacy and test your theory."

Chapter Twenty-Four

Ynya felt sick.

She barely slept all night, and getting woken up early to spar with Synol drained her of an incredible amount of energy. She still hadn't managed to recover enough to replace what she had lost, but she also couldn't bring herself to eat right now.

Ynya had spent countless hours wracking her brain over the type of magic that her mother had given her.

She had a lot of clues to go off of, but most of them hadn't started making sense until she had come here.

The ability to step outside of the Queen's constantly controlling beat was her first big clue.

The important part wasn't that she had commanded her muscles to step out of it, it was that she had managed to control her heart to step out of it.

My heart.

The same location that her mother's magic had settled. Combined with some other strangeness that had happened in the past, she thought she might know exactly what the magic was and how to use it.

Her body brimmed with anticipation at this revelation, but she needed a way to test it when the Queen wasn't around, or anyone else. She couldn't risk anyone knowing what magic she had.

"Ynya?"

Ynya looked up to the Queen's inquisitive voice.

"Is something troubling you? You haven't touched your food."

Ynya looked at the Queen.

She knows. She knows exactly what I'm thinking.

Terror spread throughout Ynya's body at the thought. All the hairs on her arms stood as goosebumps formed on her skin. Despite being quite warm, she felt incredibly cold.

"No, Your Majesty. I think I'm just not feeling well. Would it be all right if I went back to my room and tried to sleep?"

The Queen's normally hard face softened, her beady eyes taking on an almost motherly quality. "Oh, you're not feeling well? I'm sorry to hear that." She grabbed her napkin and dabbed at her mouth. The Queen's voice lost all its softness. "Of course if you had managed to actually beat your sister during one of your sparring matches, I think you would be feeling a little better about yourself."

Nervousness flitted through Ynya's mind, but she brushed it off, not wanting to betray her true emotions or thoughts. She just needed to navigate the turbulent waters of the Queen to get out of this.

"I'm sure it would have. Perhaps if I meditate on it for a bit then I might come to a conclusion?"

The Queen dropped her napkin on the table and raised

her eyebrows. "You think some introspection might help you out of the pickle you are in? You don't think I see the constant glances between you all? You think I haven't felt you use your hidden magic a few times since you got here?" She spread her arms wide. "This is my castle, and I know everything that goes on in here. I feel every bit of it. I *hear* every bit of it."

Ynya swallowed.

A growing dread rose in her mind.

Ynya's time was quickly running out. She'd been living with the Frost Queen for days now and had done nothing of worth to escape. She was becoming complacent, and the reward for complacency was readily coming due.

Ynya swallowed again. Her mouth and throat were incredibly dry. She clacked her tongue, trying to coax moisture from her mouth, but none came.

One of her fingers began to twitch and she formed a fist to try to quell the growing terror.

But the finger refused to stop.

The Queen stood from the table, kicking the chair backwards so hard that it fell over and crashed.

The barrier Ynya had tried to form broke as nervousness, worry, and fear flooded her mind, along with a tightness in her chest.

This is it. I've waited too long, and pushed her too far.

Ynya's heart pounded in her chest once again.

Lub-dub. Lub-dub.

The Queen leaned over and placed her palms on the table. The edge in her voice had been replaced with a sinister, vitriolic tongue, like a snake about to strike. "I think you are right. I think it's time we solve this little mystery once and for all."

Ynya's muscles tensed. She could still get out of this, but she needed to be careful. She glanced toward Synol.

"You think Synol will help you with this little problem?"

The Frost Queen shot out her hands with fingers spread wide. A massive frost-filled wind slammed into the room. A typhoon of power surged around Ynya. Screams filled the air as Ynya tried to see what was going on through the storm.

She built up heat in her hands as a reactionary defense move, not knowing what to expect.

The spell dissipated, and Ynya could see clearly once again.

All three of her sisters plus the Skarmyord were pinned to the wall, with thick tendrils of ice wrapped around their bodies and neck.

"Perhaps my sparring sessions haven't been enough for you. Deep in your mind you knew that it wasn't real, that it was just practice, and the worst outcome would be a reset of the room and maybe some minor healing."

The Queen narrowed her eyebrows as she curled her fingers. "I think what you need is a real-life scenario with real stakes. There is a life lesson for you here, dear Ynya. When you are forced to make a decision about someone's life, you discover things about yourself you never knew. I could try torturing you for the next couple of days, but I'm running out of time and this seems more fun."

The Queen snapped her fingers and an icy dagger appeared right in front of her, the tip buried in the wood of the table. The blade oozed a smoky blackness like it had been dipped in ink.

The Queen wrapped her hand around the handle, and pulled. The dagger came free of the table with ease. The blade hummed with a low tone as she whipped it through the air, pointing at each of the trapped individuals.

"How many do I need to kill in order to get a response out of you? Which one should I start with?"

Ynya's emotions boiled to the surface, sputtering and spattering her focus. The Queen was going to kill one of her sisters if she didn't do something! But what could she do? While she thought she knew what her mother's magic was, it had only reacted at times to save her own life. Each time it hadn't been her doing the casting, it just happened to save her life.

Her mind spun, trying to latch on to any kind of possibility.

She watched the Queen eye her blade. Maybe if she ran toward the Queen fast enough, surprising her like she had Meki, she might be able to get to her and take the dagger from her.

"You see, my dear girl, this dagger is magic, and the poison coating the blade is a particular type that only I can create or cure. It's passed down through the royal bloodline of my family as a way to protect ourselves. Usually it manifests as a reactionary magic, saving our lives at the last moment, but I've had hundreds of years to refine it and now I can pull part of it out when I need to."

She rolled the dagger around her fingers, admiring the light shining off its surfaces. "This particular poison will kill in less than a minute so you better act fast!"

The Queen spun and threw the dagger.

Ynya watched in horror as the blade buried itself deep in Synol's chest.

Chapter Twenty-Five

S ynol grunted as the dagger embedded deep in her. Her eyes glazed over as she stared into the void. A drop of blood worked out of her mouth and dribbled down her chin, reaching the end and pooling. A long string of thick blood pulled away, threatening to drip into her hands.

Ynya's mind raced as she took in the sight. *No! This can't be! What is happening?*

Deep within her chest, her heart fluttered, building up energy as an unfettered, energy built within her.

Ynya couldn't control it.

Her mother's magic flared to life, the hardness that lived within her breast surged through her body wrapping itself firmly around her heart, pumping over and over.

No longer tied to the Queen's ever-present pacing, Ynya's heart found a new rhythm. It beat entirely on its own for the first time in days. She was fully in control.

Just like it had done half a dozen times in the past, instead of her heart racing to help protect herself from harm, the magic forced her heart to slow.

The Queen clapped her hands. "Yes! There it is! I feel your hidden magic pulsing within you, Ynya.

"The poison courses through your sister's bloodstream, and soon will stop her heart forever. You have already wasted valuable time listening to me, so you might want to choose what you are going to do quickly."

The Queen narrowed her eyes. "Do you attack me, or try to protect Synol? Do you free one of your other sisters? So many choices!"

Ynya ran to Synol, heating up her hands and releasing her sister from the icy tendrils in a flash of steam and shattering ice.

She eased Synol limp body to the ground, propping her up on some chair cushions.

Their eyes met, Synol's were distant and far too soft. "Kill her, Ynya."

"No, I'm going to save you."

"Let me die, just take her out. It will be worth the sacrifice."

"No!" Ynya screamed at her sister. "I can save you!"

She had to embrace the magic fully. It was time to use her mother's gift rather than allow it to occasionally flare and save her life.

Ynya's heart pounded louder and louder, slower and slower.

Lub-dub, lub---dub.

Ynya slowed her heartbeat even more. She had control of the magic. She and the magic were finally one.

Ynya grabbed the icy dagger and yanked it from her sister's chest, tossing it to the side. The dagger shattered. Thousands of icy chunks dashed across the floor.

"I can stop this."

She placed her hands on her sister, and took a deep breath. She felt the poison under the skin, spreading deeper through Synol's body with each beat.

She had to stop Synol's heart or it would kill her.

Ynya willed her heart to slow even more. Just like it had done when Nora had thrown the dagger at the girls on the staircase. Just like the time when she had fought the woman in white back near her village and had managed to dodge the attacks of the Skarmyord to keep herself alive.

This was the magic. *This* was the secret her mother Talia Oblique had kept from them for so long.

It wasn't the ability to control the weather. It wasn't the ability to predict the future.

It was the ability to control time.

Lub–dub.

Talia Oblique's ability to control time explained so much. How she looked so young despite her age. How she was able to stay pregnant for so long with one of her children.

Lub—dub.

Time was the answer to most of her mysteries. Not all, but most, and most was good enough for now.

Pent-up magic in Ynya's hands cascaded into Synol, wrapping hard tendrils around her heart and burying itself deep into the thick, hungry muscle.

Synol's heart beat erratically as the first bits of poison poised to overwhelm her body.

"Shh, big sister. Calm yourself."

Lub-dub, lub–dub, lub—dub.

Calm. Slow. Sedate.

Ynya pushed harder, forcing her magic into Synol's heart, encasing it in a firm but gentle grip.

She could almost feel her sister's heart in her hand. The

taught, twitchy muscles recoiled from her touch, but she continued.

Lub...dub, lub......dub, lub.........dub.

Lub...

Then...nothing.

Synol's heart no longer beat.

Ynya's heart no longer beat.

All around Ynya, the room had stopped.

Ynya looked around, her mind in a haze. She felt the air thick around her, brushing against her skin as she turned her head side to side. Dust hung, suspended, defying even gravity itself, held in place by her magic.

All around the room, the hardness she'd felt for so long in her chest now held everything in place. Static, suspended, stasis.

Ynya clutched Synol in her arms, lifeless, but peaceful. Her other sisters were still attached to the wall, unmoving. Nora's eyes had frozen wide with fear as she gazed at Synol.

And the Queen. The Queen of the North, the Frost Queen herself, stood frozen in time.

This was it. This was what Ynya had been waiting for. Finally, a time when she had a leg-up on her captor.

Ynya laid Synol back down on the ground, carefully removing her hand from her sister's chest. She waited to ensure that time stayed frozen, that the poison moments away from killing Synol had not moved.

Satisfied that she didn't need to hold onto her sister any longer, Ynya stood.

Ynya pulled the golden earring from her pocket and walked up to the Queen. She halted for a moment, weighing the little object in her hand while she decided if this was the right course of action. She could go for the explosive one, but this golden one clearly was special.

It could be the one to take down the Frost Queen.

Ynya opened the earring and reached out to pierce the Queen's ear. Ynya hesitated. A hundred questions flooded her mind in a cacophony of noise and unanswered desires.

Was this the right thing to do? How much energy would I be able to maintain holding Synol in time like this? What if I took away the Queen's magic?

The Queen had said that the only one who could heal Synol was her, so if she took the woman's magic away now, she might have just doomed her own sister to death.

Ynya took a long breath, thinking through the possibilities. It was an odd feeling, not feeling your heart beat in your chest, while still having all the time in the world.

At least until you ran out of magic.

With the early morning activities, the lack of food, and the certain death of her sister, she couldn't risk killing the Queen right now.

She looked around again at the room, her mind whirling through all the actions of the day. She thought through what the Queen had told her again, dissecting the ramifications and threats.

Attacking or killing the Queen might make her feel better, but Ynya wouldn't be able to forgive herself if she traded Synol's life for that of the Queen.

Once my family is safe I will do whatever I must to ensure you never hurt anyone ever again.

Ynya put away the earring, went back to Synol, and released the spell on the rest of the room.

Chapter Twenty-Six

“Oh Ynya, Ynya, Ynya! I knew you had it within you all along! A time mage at that! Imagine the possibilities!” The Queen actually clapped with joy while Ynya caressed her limp sister's face.

Ynya barely contained her rage to not immediately attack the Queen in a futile attempt to punish her for what she had just done to Synol. “I did what you said, now release my sisters!”

The Queen stopped clapping and looked around the room. “Very well, though I have to say I'm actually quite surprised that you didn't just stop time and escape, or kill me in the process.”

“I didn't know if you were lying about being the only one who could cure her and I wasn't willing to risk her life to find out.”

The Queen's demeanor changed in a heartbeat. Her sharp-edged tongue fell right back into place. “I'm glad you understand that fact. I am the only one in the north who can cure her. I was not lying about that.”

If the Queen had noticed what Ynya was about to do to her while time had been frozen, she hadn't let on. That was good. Ynya hoped she had no memories of that moment.

Ynya stood, holding the heartbeat of her older sister still with her mother's magic. It turned out to be surprisingly easy to do so. Ynya wondered if she could only hold one thing in stasis, or if she could do multiple. She still hadn't gotten much of a test, but at least she handled the basics of the magic. Having it inside of her for the last couple months helped her understand the feel of it better. It was almost like intuition, similar to the way she held her fire magic in her hair or hands.

She needed to maintain the magic until Synol was healed.

"You promised that if we obeyed and helped you break the barrier, then you would release us and allow us to go back home?"

The Queen folded her arms and squinted. "I did say that, yes."

Ynya knelt on the cold, stone ground before the Queen. "Then I willingly submit to your assistance and will promise not to fight against you, but only if you promise that you will remove the poison from Synol. Do you accept my submission?"

The Queen pursed her lips, the corner of her mouth curling up in a sinister smile. "Ynya, darling, you pain me in your request. Of course I do. I promise, as the Frost Queen of the North herself, that once the Feond is down, I will cure your sister of the poison and allow all of you to return home unharmed."

That was about as much of a promise that Ynya was going to get from the Queen. She wanted to push for an immediate resolution, but the risk to Synol was too great. The Queen had already demonstrated she was willing to risk lives to get what she wanted.

For a moment, Ynya considered freeing time once again and attempting to kill the Queen.

Maybe I can find someone else who can cure Synol.

Regardless, she didn't believe a word from the bitch's mouth and would still do everything she could to figure out a means of escape.

"One more thing," Ynya stated. "You cannot ask any of us to do anything that would put Synol's life in jeopardy. If you force me to release my hold on her heart to stop time on something else, then you have to cure her in order for me to do so."

The Queen snarled, showing off her teeth. "I could just kill her now so you don't have the distraction."

Ynya drew her lips to a line as the rage she was so familiar with bubbled to the surface once again. "Then it will be the last spell you cast." Ynya took a threatening step toward the woman, hands balled into overheated fists. "You need us alive for your plans to work, don't you? You have a choice. Honor your commitments and keep us safe, or turn us against you. If you try to take it all from us by force, we will fight against you to our last breath."

Ynya pointed at her youngest sister. "I know Meki is more powerful than you, I feel it every time you draw magic from her. I also know how you control Finny's magic, but you need both of them for whatever you have planned. Synol might not have been absolutely necessary for your plan, but now that you know what magic I have within me, you won't risk losing it."

Ynya balled her hands, pouring heat into them so hard that her fingernails glowed with red heat. "So I ask once more, do you agree or not?"

Ynya was done playing around with the woman. She knew she could stop time again at any point and put the earring on the Queen while keeping Synol in stasis, so she still had that in case the Queen decided to go back on her promises.

The Queen snapped her fingers. Released from their icy prisons, Finny, Meki, and Nora crumpled to the ground.

Ynya looked at each of them.

Nora glared back with a small nod of thanks, but darted her concerned gaze back to Synol.

Meki sat on the ground, her face buried in her hands, crying.

Finny never took her eyes off the Frost Queen, wearing an unbridled angry scowl only a young girl could muster.

Ynya frowned. The Queen hadn't exactly relented, but she had complied. It would have to be good enough for now.

Ynya sat down at the table to get back enough power to keep Synol alive.

Chapter Twenty-Seven

✦

"Again!"

Ynya closed her eyes as she breathed in the cold mid-day air. It wasn't fair forcing her to have to practice sparring against Nora so soon after Synol had almost died.

But the Queen doesn't seem to care about Synol living or dying.

Of course she didn't. All the Queen cared about was obtaining more power. She would do anything for that power, would sacrifice anything to get it.

The Queen insisted the sparring session take place out in the open air in front of the castle in the rock.

Ynya didn't care, as long as nothing hurt Synol. In fact, it was kind of nice to be out under the sky once again. Ynya spent most of her life out in the open, given her ability to withstand even the most frigid of temperatures. Being inside meant she overheated too easily, and she missed the freedom of being out in the open.

Not that being forced to fight your aunt was much of a freedom.

At least the sky was relatively clear this afternoon.

Nora stood above her, holding out a hand.

Ynya hesitated before taking it. There was no sense worrying if the Skarmyord was going to hurt her anymore. The way Nora had looked on in terror at Synol was telling. Whatever had happened in that room had clearly affected her long-lost aunt. Ynya didn't know why Nora suddenly had concern for their well-being, but Ynya would take any sympathy she could get at this point.

Nora yanked hard, pulling Ynya to her feet in a jolt. Ynya slammed into Nora's chest with a leathery thump, her head bumping into Nora's shoulder. The action knocked the wind out of her lungs.

"I'll help you escape," Nora whispered. She let go and walked away like nothing had happened.

What was that?

Ynya watched the woman walk away, her thoughts swirling around her as she struggled to get her spasming lungs to respond.

She was impressed. That was a sneaky way of passing on a message.

Nora took her stance about twenty paces away, baring both hands with daggers. "You heard Her Highness. Are you ready?"

***

It was a long, frustrating, and exhausting day. Ynya felt like falling into the bed and sleeping everything off, but...*What if my spell stops while I'm asleep?*

Power from her magic seeped from Ynya into her immobile sister. It was significantly faster than her normal self-heating spells, so Ynya found she had to consume a significant amount of food to overcome the constant drain. Rest would help, but Ynya wasn't willing to try that yet.

She tried to think back to the times when her mother had used the magic, but she couldn't note anything specific. Synol had been the oldest, and might remember some times when Talia had used her time magic in front of the kids without worrying about them being old enough to remember.

Unfortunately, Synol was near to death, and Ynya wasn't willing to wake her just to ask her to scour her memories in hopes that Ynya could glean a bit more information about their now-deceased mother.

The whole situation wore on her mind. It was all Ynya could do to keep from falling apart. Her mother and father were dead, Synol was seconds away from death, and Ynya was forced to spend her days training under the tutelage of a tyrant Queen.

She held onto the seething rage toward the Queen, keeping it close. Sometimes it was the only thing preventing her from bawling her eyes out.

The three sisters carefully placed Synol into the middle of the large bed.

Ynya was surprised how easy it had been for her to maintain the spell from outside the castle while Synol stayed inside. She suspected that was another test from the Queen, checking to see if Ynya could do it. Again, driving home the fact that the Queen truly didn't care about them, she only wanted their magic for her purposes. If Synol died as part of her test, then it wouldn't be anything to worry over.

But it would be one she would regret.

A pall hung over the girls as they prepared for bed, one that Ynya couldn't hold back anymore. She knew they were being watched, but things needed to be said, and since Synol wasn't able to say them, Ynya needed to pick up the mantle.

"We will make it out of here, I promise."

Meki, who had been silent all day looked up at her with her big eyes. "You think so?"

Finny huffed. "I'm telling you, the Queen is lying."

"I know that, Finny," Ynya replied, pushing down irritation at the callous way Finny spoke.

Ynya beckoned Meki over to her and held her tightly in her lap. It felt so good to have her little sister in her arms. She wished Finny would join, but Finny had changed. She wasn't much of a hugger before, but definitely wasn't now. She seemed more preoccupied with the monster in the basement than anything else in her life.

Stop. It's not her fault.

Ynya knew it wasn't her fault, but she had so much anger pent up in her now that she just needed a place to release it. The non-stop sparring had helped keep her mind off their plight most of the day, but ever since dinner, with nothing to punch, Ynya's fists were getting antsy.

Ynya had to remind herself that Finny had been through more than any of them had. So young, yet so much pain, so much heartache. None of it was fair, and yet Finny seemed to be holding herself together as best she could.

Possibly better than me.

Mostly, Ynya wished they could all be hugged by Synol.

After calming her strained voice, Ynya replied to Finny. "I know the Queen lied to us, but until we know exactly why or how, there is little sense worrying about it. All we can do is keep each other close, and remain constantly vigilant about our own safety."

"She intends for you to fight Pain and I tomorrow." Finny

said, sitting down on the bed. For a second she looked over to Synol's time-stopped body and even extended her hand in a half-attempt to hold Synol's, but Finny retracted it just as fast.

Ynya noticed, however, and it warmed her heart knowing that the sweet Finny she once knew was still in there somewhere.

"I was wondering where you had been all day."

"She had me...training down in the kennels." Finny pulled her knees to her chest and wrapped her arms around her legs.

Ynya swallowed, remembering the overwhelming smell of animals last time she had been down there. "What sort of things do I need to know?"

Finny looked away. "We're both...she made me change... and we ate...and..."

"Ate some of the animals? It's okay, Finny. I know she forces you both to do certain things. Do you know what she intends for you to do, Finny? Why is she having you and Pain learn to fight?"

Finny's stare seemed to linger on the door before snapping back to reality.

"She needs us to help fight through the Feond. It's the same reason she linked herself to Meki's frost magic, to boost her own abilities. I don't know exactly, but once she's made it through the other side of the barrier, I don't think she's letting any of us go."

Ynya nodded. She had figured that. She knew the Queen hadn't been truthful in her promises, but Ynya chose to hold onto that promise while also planning for the worst. *Anything to keep up hope was a good thing, right?*

Still, fighting meant death, and death meant they wouldn't be able to go home. Helping the Queen get past the barrier, even assuming she followed through with her promise of letting them go, didn't mean they were going to make it home safe.

Ynya needed more information. She needed to know exactly what the Queen had in store for them. She needed to find out more about the Feond. She needed to talk to Nora.

Chapter Twenty-Eight

❧❧❧

After putting the others to bed, Ynya slowly opened the door from their room.

The floor above them held the Queen's study and that rune on the large stone. Ynya felt waves of magic surging up above her. Bigger and smaller, back and forth.

The Queen was definitely up to something.

Ynya wanted to sneak up and spy on the activities, perhaps find something in the room that would help her break the curse on Synol. Due to the thrum of magic through the frigid air, Ynya suspected the Queen prepared her spells for passage through the Feond.

The hallway was surprisingly devoid of any guards. Nora had told that she would be watching the door all night, so where was she?

Their extremely brief one-sided conversation from earlier ran over and over in her mind. Ynya still wasn't sure what Nora meant by that.

Ynya hesitated before stepping out into the hallway. Had Nora cleared the hallways of any other guards so that she could run? Did Nora want her to make a run for it tonight, or was it all a test to see if Ynya and her sisters would try to take the opportunity to escape?

Thoughts swirled around in Ynya's head while she went posited just how she was going to get away from the Queen and her army. She wasn't going to leave anyone behind, so that meant they would have to carry Synol on their own.

Carrying Synol meant they would be slow, and being slow meant they needed to create plenty of distance between themselves and the Queen.

That meant they either needed to sneak out in the dead of night before anyone noticed, or Ynya would need to what... stop time?

For how long? For how large of an area? Am I supposed to halt time on the entire army while we trudge through the snow half-dead? How much power would that even use?

A shudder jolted through her shoulders at the thought. She wasn't sure she could stop time for that long, for the entire castle or army. She managed to stop time effectively enough in the room with the Queen earlier, but had that stopped it all for the whole castle? It had also drained her quite a bit to do that, and that was just a handful of people in a single room.

She couldn't handle three-thousand spread across a huge open plain.

Without more in-depth testing to this new magic, she didn't know what she was capable of, but she wasn't willing to do anything if it meant jeopardizing her sister's life.

Still, leaving the castle and pissing off the Queen seemed like a bad idea if the Queen was the only one to be able to save Synol.

"Ynya! What are you doing out of the room?"

Ynya froze at Nora's question. The Skarmyord seemed to appear out of nowhere!

Nora held the all-too-familiar silver dagger to Ynya's back. "I told you not to leave the room. You are being watched at *all* times."

Ynya noticed the emphasis on the word *all*. Nora had to be putting on a show for someone.

Ynya didn't know if she could fully trust her aunt, but at this point, she didn't have much of a choice. She needed answers, and Nora was the only one she could possibly get them from.

Worst-case, the Queen probably already knew that Ynya plotted escape, so even if word got back to the Queen, it wouldn't put them in any worse of a situation.

Ynya chose her words carefully, in case other ears listened to their interaction. "I needed some food. I'm starving from all the fighting today and having to maintain the spell on my sister. I only opened the door looking for you but you weren't here, so I waited."

Nora huffed quietly. "Very well, I will escort you downstairs for some food, but someone will guard this door to ensure no one else leaves or comes in."

Less than a second later, a burly guard materialized from the wall a few yards away.

Ynya shuddered at the notion that he had been so close that whole time but hadn't been visible. She was right to "play the game" like Synol had told her to.

Nora dug the dagger into her back as she directed Ynya down the hallway.

Instead of heading to the dining room or kitchen, Nora instead led Ynya down a series of hallways and back-stairs.

Before she knew it, they were out in the animal area.

Nora checked around the corner, then finally spoke.

"You could have gotten yourself killed. You have to be *very* careful."

Ynya narrowed her eyes. Before she was going to engage in any conversation with this woman, she needed to know where her aunt's loyalties lay.

"What you told me earlier, what did you mean by that? Are you helping us escape?"

Nora glanced around again, an angry look on her face. "We're going to be caught, I should get you back. This was a mistake."

Ynya grabbed her aunt's hand, cupping it against her chest. The Skarmyord's hands were cold and rough. "No. This is right. I have an aunt that I never knew until recently, and I just need to know if she's looking out for me and my sisters. That's all I want."

Nora looked into Ynya's eyes. Her face was frighteningly gaunt, and her eyes fierce, reminding Ynya of being scolded by her mother as a young girl.

The brief memory pained Ynya.

After a long stare, Nora softened her shoulders and looked away. "Seeing Synol stabbed like that was like reliving something similar with Talia. When you told me your mother had died by my soldier's hand, memories I thought I'd long-since buried bubbled up, taking hold of my heart and not letting go. I've been fighting them ever since. It was why I let you go when you escaped back in the caravan, and allowed Synol to leave with her husband to find you."

"You let us go back then? I thought I escaped?"

Ignoring the question, Nora placed her free hand on Ynya's and squeezed. "Your mother was so determined, strong, but so sweet in everything she did. She was the one who escaped Reyoarfjell and she came back, but I betrayed her to the Warden and nearly got her killed. I abandoned her in her time of need and forced her to have to escape twice.

"Even with all my Enlightenment training, I never forgave my betrayal and I always hoped she had survived. It was... surprising when my family's name came up on a list so many years later.

"I couldn't believe she had kept our surname, and that your father took it for his own. I really thought she would have changed her name a dozen times in order to hide."

Nora dropped Ynya's hands to peek around the corner again. Seemingly satisfied, she came back.

"Look, we can catch up later if you really want, but for now, you need to know what the Queen has in store for you."

Ynya nodded her head. "That's why I opened the door. Something is going on and I don't know what to do."

Chapter Twenty-Nine

"The first thing you need to know is that the Queen isn't exactly human," Nora said.

"You mean her pointed ears? I assume she's an elf?" Even though elves had been a superstition passed down as stories, the fact that they were real didn't surprise Ynya.

Nora nodded. "Yes, the race of elves live far to the south. A few hundred years ago, they started fighting among themselves. No one knows exactly why the fighting started, but it ended up turning into a civil war between the Queen and her father, the king of the elves. The Queen's brother sided with her, and together they started an uprising against her tyrant king."

Ynya huffed. "So she learned her tyranny from her father?"

Nora let out a small smile, but turned that into a grimace instead. "This is all rumor passed down over the centuries. Remember all we know is what the Queen herself has shared or distant memories from humans who lived through it long ago. I don't think anyone truly knows what happened, but regardless, there was a huge battle long ago where she killed her own mother, sending the father into grief and turning the tide of the battle.

"But in-doing so, she unwittingly released a huge amount of magic that was ultimately used against her. The king killed his own son, and mortally injured his daughter, then chased her up here into the frozen north where she went into hiding.

"Rather than try to hunt her down, the King erected a huge barrier called the Feond, to keep her locked away. Unfortunately, the barrier also sealed a large number of humans up here with her, cutting us off from trade with the kingdoms to the south.

"Eventually, she recovered, and her power grew, but she was never so powerful as she was before. She lost something in that battle, something that permanently hindered her powers. She thinks that once she takes down the Feond, she'll be able to regain full-use of her powers to take back the throne from her father."

Ynya took it all in, trying to read between the lines of ancient history to see how it all fit together with the Queen's plans for them. "So that's why she has a standing army out front of the castle? She means to take down the Feond and go to battle against her father?"

Nora pursed her lips and shook her head. "Not exactly. The army consists of magic-wielding soldiers who have been through Reyoarfjell. Not quite Skarmyord, but close. She keeps their magic locked down for the most part, but if you pay close attention while walking through the camp, you can feel it humming in the background. She's not going to use them for fighting."

"Then what?" Ynya asked, a bit of worry creeping into her mind at the baited question.

Nora drew in a sharp breath and let it out slowly. Her nostrils flared just like Talia Oblique's, Ynya dead mother.

"She's going to kill them all for their power."

"She's what?" Ynya's chest tightened so suddenly, she felt like she couldn't breathe. Thousands of soldiers all being collected into one area suddenly made sense. If the Queen sacrificed them all for their power, she could use that power to cast a huge spell.

"Then, that's why she wants us?"

Nora nodded. "Once her entire army is killed, she will still need someone to fight for her."

"That's why she holding onto Finny and..." Ynya trailed off as she looked through walls to where the monster formerly known as Firtze sat in his cage.

All the clues Finny had been dropping about her relation-ship with the monster she called Pain surged through Ynya's mind. She wasn't just a friend of this monster, she was in love! She wanted to spend time with him because of the changes the Queen's scientists had done to her.

"She's breeding monsters to use for her army?"

Nora nodded. "Until you disrupted and destroyed her operations at Reyoarfjell, yes. Despite your interruption, the Queen has two of those beasts now, so she is hoping to breed them to create an army."

Ynya stood, stunned at the revelation. "Poor Finny."

Nora grunted her agreement.

"Wait," Ynya realized something, "then what about the rest of us?"

Nora ground her teeth for a moment before replying. "Her sacrificing Synol was not something I expected her to do, given

Synol's immense earth powers. I think she took a gamble that your—or maybe, Talia's—magic was worth the risk. She might be banking on you keeping her alive until she gets what she wants from you, then curing Synol. Or maybe she'll kill her, I don't rightly know and there is no way to tell what her ultimate plans are for each of you.

"Remember that book of charts she showed you? She back-tracked through it once she learned all your powers, and surmised what magic Talia probably had, but she still needed to test to be sure."

Ynya stopped breathing for a moment. "So she knew all-along what magic I had?"

Nora nodded, her eyes wistful as she peered through her past memories.

"Your mother was an absolute miracle. No-one is born with time magic but once every five-thousand years. Remember Her Majesty's book, the one that documents a five-thousand history? The entire cycle is centered around the birth of one with time magic. Your mother knew how much of a value her magic was, so she would have done everything possible to pass it on to someone she trusted. If the Queen knew what your mother was, she knew Talia would have passed it on to either you or Synol. You not expending all of your magic during battles told the Queen that you probably had it."

Nora stopped talking for a second. The tension in the small hallway had grown to such a fever pitch that Ynya couldn't hold her emotions in check any more.

Ynya hadn't known that her new-found magic was so rare. She was an idiot to not think of it. Stopping time? Was she daft? What magic could *possibly* be more powerful than being able to stop time? This made what her mother did so much more poignant to Ynya, making her realize just how much her mother planned their births.

In a burst of emotion, Ynya wrapped her arms around Nora and squeezed. "I miss Mama so much. I'm sorry about the way I threw it in your face when we first met."

Nora, after a few seconds, returned the hug, though Ynya could tell she hadn't hugged anyone in a very long time with the awkward way she responded. "It's something I would have done, use my own pain as a weapon. You are I are a lot alike in that aspect. It was something I...respected about you when we first met."

Nora stepped back, holding Ynya at arm's length. "But the reality is that Finny will be bred for an army of those...things... while you and Meki will either be drained of your power, or forced to gift your powers to her. Most likely the second for both of you."

"Gift?"

Nora nodded her head. "Yes, it's quite painful, and usually leaves you dead at the end, which is why Talia held on for so long until you returned. She must have stopped time for herself until you arrived. Her magic was too powerful to just allow it to go back to the Concordance, but now that the Queen knows you have it and are here, she's never going to let you go. She will have yours and Meki's magics. Best case, she will cure Synol and force her to gift her magic just like the rest, or sacrifice her for the same cause."

"And Finny will not have any sort of free life ever?"

Nora didn't reply, but the tension in the hall told Ynya everything she needed to know.

Despite the dour conversation, Ynya's mind was sharp, and focused on the tasks at hand. She shoved her hands in her pocket to feel the three earrings latched onto the fabric of her dress while the beginnings of a plan began to sprout in her mind. She pondered asking her aunt what the gold earring did, but wanted to talk to her sisters first, just in case Nora was still telling her these things under orders of the Queen.

"That leaves only one question, how do we get out of here?"

Chapter Thirty

Ynya slowly chewed on her fourth roll for breakfast the next morning.

The Queen hadn't called for anyone to battle yet, which was good, as Ynya hadn't slept all night.

What she had done was work out a rough plan in her head, and come clean to her sisters about the earrings and the Queen's plans for them.

Talking so openly in their room was a gamble for sure, but Nora had insisted that the Queen was so confident in her hold over everyone in the castle, that she didn't have anyone else but Nora and one other guard watching the room.

Nora supposedly took care of that guard when she and Ynya returned to the sisters' room.

That allowed Ynya to spend the night with her sisters free of the worry that they were being watched.

It felt amazing being able to talk to each of them in turn the way she wished she had this whole time. Meki in particular turned out to be quite chatty and grateful for all the attention Ynya had given her since she arrived.

They hugged, cried, planned, and schemed.

They knew what they were going to do.

Today was the day, now all Ynya needed to do was wait for the perfect opportunity.

The Queen entered the dining hall, projecting her immense magic to drop the temperature of the room by a couple of degrees before entering.

A stealthy rogue, she was not. She truly was so sure of her magic that there was no doubt where she roamed.

The Queen stopped in the doorway as she took in the room.

"What is *she* doing here?" The Queen gestured to Synol, now propped up in the chair next to Ynya.

Ynya narrowed her eyes and folded her arms to punctuate her attitude. "Synol is our sister, and if I am forced to maintain my hold on her to keep her from dying, then she will go everywhere with me until that happens."

The Queen frowned, but stepped over to her chair nonetheless. "We will see about that. As soon as we are done eating, I have something new for you all to try. I'm in my final preparations for unlocking the magic that will allow me to take down the Feond, so I need to begin training you three in your parts."

Finny coughed, which caught Ynya's attention. She looked over to see Finny's eyes wide with alarm. Finny squinted and did the hand gesture for Ynya to pay attention.

Ynya did, feeling out with her magic to sense any changes in the environment. Sure enough, something was different about the hallway; a distinct signature that she hadn't felt in a while.

Oh no.

The Queen had brought up the beast known as Pain, who sat in the hallway now along with a handful of other guards.

His presence meant one thing. There was no more time to prepare, regardless of how much time Ynya thought she had left.

Glancing to Finny again, knowing how she felt about this beast, Ynya noticed the fear on her sister's face.

Ynya needed a distraction, and a way to begin her plan immediately. It might have already been too late, but she had to try. Ynya would not submit without a fight to the death. "Perhaps Your Majesty would feel like removing the poison from my sister so we can better serve you?"

The Queen stopped eating and, without looking at anyone in particular, smiled. "My, my, you have quite the imagination, young Ynya, quite the imagination indeed. You obviously know that I have something special prepared for you, so you hope to get your sister back before that?"

The Queen dropped the sausage she was about to eat onto her plate, then dusted her hands. "The reality is that I don't need your sister's powers. She was never the one I cared about. Earth mages can certainly be useful, and she definitely has an immense amount of power behind her. But you see, earth magic is quite useless when you have goals such as mine. It requires too much of a sacrifice to use and drawing out your time magic was the reason I sacrificed her anyway."

The Queen pushed back from the table and stood, licking her lips. "No, dear Ynya, the reality is that Synol was your mother's first experiment, and she was still learning when she had her. Each of you has more unique and specialized powers than the last one. Synol has raw power, sure, but the rest of you have something else locked within you that I intend to utilize.

Something else locked within us? What did you do, Mama?

"I don't need her distracting you anymore." The Queen raised a hand and snapped.

Ynya thrust her magic out in a massive burst to stop time for everyone in the room.

Ynya turned. Sure enough, five large ice spikes materialized in the air above Synol, with the largest less than two inches from Synol's head.

Fear gripped Ynya's chest as she realized how casually the Queen had planned to end Synol's life.

Ynya channeled that fear into rage toward the evil Queen and built up heat in her hands.

In one swift motion, Ynya smashed all of the ice spikes hurtling toward her sister, then dragged Synol's chair to the wall, ensuring Synol was well out of the zone from getting hurt.

This was it, this was the time for fighting and running.

Ynya had spent the night munching on as much food as she could, knowing that she would need to store up power for today.

But regardless of how much power she had built up, holding onto the time drained her more than any fire she used.

Ynya glanced around the room. Finny and Meki's mouths both hung open halfway, having only recognized what was going to happen before time stopped.

The Queen wore a dastardly grin on her too-thin face, and Nora stood against the wall with her arms folded, a stoic but grim look on her face.

Ynya reached into her pocket, pulling out the three earrings stored within, and looked at them, trying to determine which one to use against the Queen.

As Ynya herself had demonstrated, the silver one was easily defeated by simply ripping it out of your ear. Gross and painful, but worth getting your magic back. It wouldn't work on the Queen.

The bronze one exploded if you tried ripping it out, so that might be an effective method of locking down the Queen's magic.

But Ynya suspected the Queen probably had ways to get that one out.

That left the golden earring. The Warden had tried to convince Ynya to put that on herself, so it clearly did something, but what? *I should have asked Nora about the earrings last night! Why hadn't I asked about them?*

It was now or never. Ynya needed to make a decision.

Everything they were doing now was a gamble, so Ynya jabbed the Queen's ear with the golden earring, and started time up again.

Chapter Thirty-One

A s soon as time started, the remaining chunks of ice that Ynya broke slammed into the ground right where Synol's lifeless body had been.

Ynya hesitated, her gaze never leaving the Queen's in order to suss out exactly what the earring had done to the Frost Queen of the North.

Ynya readied herself to stop time once again in case the earring didn't do its job.

The Queen gasped, and both hands went for her ear as she realized what Ynya had also done.

Whew.

Ynya smiled. "I'm sorry, Your Highness, but I don't think we can take you up on your offer today. In fact, we are going to leave this place right now."

The Queen's gaze didn't leave Ynya's for what seemed an eternity, but her shocked expression finally softened, and eventually, the Queen's mouth turned upward into a broad smile.

"Oh, my dear. I thought for a second that you had used the bronze one on me, that would have actually done some damage, but wouldn't have killed me. This one, however, was made for humans."

The Queen took a step toward Ynya. "You see, sometimes, when we are torturing you to bring out your magics, they come out too fast. Uncontrolled magic is a very dangerous thing, so this golden earring was designed to immediately void all magic in a human. It almost always kills the host, but at least you don't have to deal with the collateral damage. It can be quite catastrophic when it happens."

The Queen blinked, and Ynya saw a flash of burned and mangled flesh on the right side of the Queen's body. The Queen blinked again and it was gone. "I know just how dangerous uncontrolled magic can be, young one, so I made sure that we had a way to contain it."

The Queen reached up and rubbed a bony finger over the gold earring. "Unfortunately, magic works differently for my kind then it does for you, so this has no effect on me. You can thank my father for that."

The Queen grabbed the earring, pouring frost magic into it, then twisted.

In a high-pitched *ping*, the earring shattered into three parts, falling to the floor.

The Queen smiled once again. Her toothy grin terrified Ynya to her core.

Shit!

The Queen whistled, and Pain bounded in from the hallway. His ears were back and bristles on high-alert. His milky eyes took in the scene, landing and lingering on Ynya.

Finny yelled. "Ynya!"

Ynya watched in horror as Finny's body twisted and contorted in on itself.

Black lines formed over her body, filling in her pale skin as her bones shifted and re-sorted themselves into a creature that stood on all fours.

Instead of red-haired Finny, a beast near-identical to Pain leapt atop the table.

The Queen whistled, and both beasts bounded in one easy jump to stand on either side of their master.

They sniffed and growled at each other.

Ynya looked between the two, not sure how to react. Should she stop time for everyone but her sisters? Should she stop time for everyone and personally carry everyone out? Could she take out the Queen with her fire magic while inside the time bubble?

"Now that my two pets are here, it's time for us to begin. I really wish things didn't have to end this way, Ynya, but I will have to take your magic from you until I'm ready to perform the proper rituals."

Ynya's magic disappeared once again, just like it had done out on the frozen plains when they had first arrived.

"No!" Ynya yelled. Once again, the void in her chest was like a gaping wound in her soul when she didn't have access to her magic.

Behind her, Synol gasped.

Hearing that gut-wrenching sound tore Ynya's heart in two.

"Synol!" Ynya turned to run toward her sister, but the larger of the two monsters, Pain, growled and leapt on top of Ynya, knocking her to the floor. Thick talons scratched her back through the fabric of her dress, drawing blood.

Finny roared.

Half a second later, Finny barreled into Pain, knocking him off of Ynya.

Ynya rolled as the two snapped and growled at each other.

"Enough!" The Queen screamed, "I need her taken alive!"

The two beasts ignored the Queen, snapping and snarling at each other. They paced around in a circle, their eyes never leaving one another.

The Queen narrowed her eyes. "You will both obey me!"

Finny looked over at the Queen and spoke. Her voice was hoarse and scratchy, but it was definitely Finny. "You will not control me anymore, false Queen. You have no pull over my magic when I am in this form. You should have thought about that when you had them make me. You control him no better, like a dog, and dogs can turn on their masters."

The Queen's face scrunched up in a contorted rage, and she pulled in magic to release in a torrent of frost. But Finny launched herself at the Queen's neck.

The Queen sidestepped, blasting Finny with a frost spell and sending her reeling against the wall.

Finny hit the stone with a grunted whine, crumpling to the ground in a heap.

Alarmed, Pain bounded over to her, whimpering.

Ynya's face filled with tears over how fast things had escalated. She now no-longer had access to her magic, Synol was dying, and now Finny was hurt!

Fuck!

She should have used the bronze earring on the Queen, or she should have just tried to kill the Queen with fire magic while she still had time stopped.

Pain nudged Finny with his snout while he whined. It was a sweet gesture during a time of depravity and anguish.

"I said attack, or I will do the same to you!" The Queen snarled at the beasts.

Finny got up, holding up her back leg, and turned on the Queen, growling.

Pain joined his mate in growling. Together, they paced slowly toward the Queen.

The Queen never flinched. "Very well. It seems you two need more obedience training. No matter. There will be plenty of time when I can ensure your loyalty once I have my prize." She raised her arms and cages of ice sprung up from the floor, trapping both beasts within them.

Finny and Pain threw themselves at the thick ice bars to no effect. Their bites tried but failed to grab onto the slick ice.

Ynya scrambled backwards, taking Synol in her arms.

Synol was near-death, her chest barely moving with labored breaths. Black lines wound under her skin, as the poison filled her veins.

"Synol! I'm sorry!"

"Enough!" The Queen yelled. "You will gift me your power now, or I will take it from you. If you do it now, before your sister dies, I will spare her life by removing the poison."

Chapter Thirty-Two

Ynya looked across the room at her sisters. One was trapped in ice, another was in her arms, moments away from dying by poison, and the other had her magic inexorably linked to the Queen's.

Ynya's own magic had been taken from her, so she couldn't stop time anymore. She was out of options.

Her heart ached at having to make a decision such as this, but she had no choice. She couldn't allow any of her sisters to be harmed or killed, regardless of how it affected her, or however much power it gave the Queen.

She would always choose her sisters.

"Very well, but I want you to remove the poison from Synol first. I can't have her dying while I do this."

The Queen frowned. "You are in no position to demand anything from me, but since you came to a decision so quickly, I will reverse the progress."

The Queen snapped her fingers, and Synol sat up more. Her eyes brightened, and she looked around the room with a new vigor. Her mottled skin regained most of her color, and the poisoned lines all but disappeared.

"She now has a couple minutes, so you better hurry."

"What do I need to do? Can I even gift it with my magic taken from me?"

The Queen nodded. "Your magic is still there, you are just prevented from using it yourself. I left just enough of an opening for you to gift it. Look inside yourself, feel for your magic, then look behind it, look for a link to the Concordance deep in the back. Follow that thread as far as you can. There, you will be able to detach your magic thread and gift it to me."

The Queen knelt down. "You must use both of your hands to hold my head in order to gift it, but you must do so willingly. If you do not, if you do not mean to gift me your magic, then it will fail. If you fail, your sister dies and I will be forced to take it from you."

"Take it?" Ynya's jaw trembled at the thought.

"Yes, I can take your magic from you, but the process damages the magic in the transfer. It will never be as powerful or as pure as if it was gifted. So, you can see I would prefer you gift it. Are you ready for this?"

Of course Ynya wasn't ready for this, but did she have a choice? She couldn't do anything that would put Synol's life at risk. Even now, Synol's seconds ticked by and there was no guarantee that the Queen would actually save her life.

Ynya looked inside her, at the place where her magic lived. Sure enough, her magics were there, but not powered. Touching them, she felt the distant hum of her fire, and beside it, Talia's time magic slowly drummed to her heartbeat.

"Very well."

"Your Highness." Nora spoke up. "She still has a bronze earring on her and could use it against you."

The Queen turned slightly sideways toward Nora. "Very keen observation. I knew there was a reason I kept you around. Ynya, hand those earrings to the Captain so they can be destroyed."

Ynya reached into her pocket and handed the earrings to her aunt, who took them without meeting her gaze. Nora seemed to know exactly what she was planning, and not for the first time this morning, Ynya wondered exactly where Nora's loyalties were.

She had seemed amiable and almost lovable the night before, giving her all sorts of information, but Ynya wondered if that was all part of the plan. Perhaps the Queen had told her to allow Ynya to entertain her thoughts of escape.

This must have been why the Queen showed up with the dogs this morning. Nora must have told her about the questions Ynya had been asking.

It made sense. Ynya scowled at her retreating aunt. She would deal with her later. Right now, she had to save Synol.

Ynya reached inside of her once again, feeling for her magic, then stepped over to the Queen.

The Queen smiled at her, an almost-genuine smile this time. "You are making the right decision here, Ynya. Your mother would be proud."

Ynya hesitated.

Would she?

Talia Oblique had entrusted Ynya to rescue her sisters from the Frost Queen, and here was Ynya doing exactly opposite of what she had promised her mother.

"No!" Ynya yelled, balling her fists up and putting them down by her sides. "My mother would NOT be proud if she could see me now. She would be angry. She entrusted me with her magic and told me to rescue my sisters."

The Queen frowned. "That is too bad. I guess I will restart the poison in your sister once again."

Ynya turned to Synol. "I'm sorry, big sis, but giving the magic to her isn't going to help us escape. She'll just have more power over us."

Synol, weak, but seemingly happy, smiled back. "It's okay, Ynya. I'm proud of you. Mother would be proud of you for standing up to her."

The Queen raised her hand, but as she did, her eyes went wide with alarm, and her body jerked three times in rapid succession.

"I cannot allow that." Nora said, wielding her silver blade next to the Queen's throat. Black lines just like the poison in Synol wormed from her hand up her forearm. "It is time that I do something noble for my family."

Chapter Thirty-Three

"You idiot!" The Queen whirled on Nora. "You know those don't work on me!"

"Not fully, but it weakens your magic and makes it easier to fight you. Now Ynya can use part of her magic to save Synol."

Inside her, Ynya felt the stirrings of her heat. The stabbing of the Queen had indeed given her back a tiny thread of magic. She turned to face Synol, who struggled to breathe as the poison took hold of her once again. "I will save you Synol, I promise."

Ynya touched her sister, using the entirety of her small thread of magic to stop Synol's heartbeat again.

The Queen thrust her hand out, grabbing Nora by the throat. "And here I thought you had finally seen the error of your ways. That is fine, I meant to take some of the people down off the wall, so clearly it is time for you to take their place."

The Queen poured magic into the Skarmyord, freezing her from the outside in.

"Leave her alone!"

Meki jumped on top of the table, a fierce look in her eyes.

The Queen whirled, Nora's neck in her hand. "What do you think you're doing, girl? Don't forget that I control your magic."

"Maybe so, but you also forgot to teach me the simple fact that a magical link goes two ways. Maybe you thought I was too young to understand, or maybe you just wanted my more powerful frost magic. It's a good thing my aunt taught me the true extent of how bonds work!"

Meki pulled in a huge amount of magic, sucking it away from the Frost Queen.

The Queen dropped Nora, whose frost-covered face had turned purple. Black lines snaked up the Captain's arm now. Clearly the Queen hadn't been lying about the protective magic in her bloodline.

Nora hit the stone floor with a thud. Her body stiffened and her eyes glazed over. Ynya needed heat to thaw out her Aunt, but before she could summon enough, a blast of cold from Meki threw the Queen into the cage containing Finny and Pain. Ynya jumped back from the blast.

The cage shattered as the Queen's limp body smashed through it.

Both beasts leapt out, snarling and hissing, snapping and clawing at the Queen as she sailed over their heads and hit the wall.

The Queen slid across the floor, but recovered quickly. She rolled to her knees and thrust out her hands, throwing a dozen spikes at Meki.

Meki guarded by crossing her arms in front of her. Ice grew across her arms in an instant, and the spikes crashed into the makeshift shield, shattering into hundreds of pieces.

One, however, missed the shield and dug into her shoulder.

Meki grunted and fell down. She grabbed the spike and ripped it from her shoulder. "You will leave my sisters alone!"

Meki pulled in an immense amount of magic once again.

Ynya felt the surge in magic flow from the Queen to Meki, showing that yes, the link between the two went both ways.

Both beasts leapt at the Queen from two different angles, but the Queen shot spikes at them. This time, however, the spikes were smaller, with less force. Each one bounced off the beasts, slowing them down, but not harming them.

Whatever Meki was doing seemed to be working.

Ynya felt more of her magic return with every massive pull Meki did.

Meki threw spikes of her own, but instead of hitting the Queen directly, they slammed around her, encasing her in an icy prison.

The Queen blasted the ice away, throwing her arms out and screaming as she did so. "You are all going to regret what you have done to me this day!"

All the action between Meki and the Queen had weakened the hold the Queen had on Ynya's magic, and she now was able to fully maintain the time freeze on Synol while also having access to some heat. It wasn't enough to incapacitate someone, but it should be enough to help her aunt.

Ynya rushed over to Nora's half-frozen body, dragging her back out of harm's way. As she did so, she poured what heat she could afford into her Aunt's body, trying to warm up the woman from the Queen's prior attacks.

The dark lines crossing her skin were bad, the poison had seeped into every bit of her body. If Ynya could freeze time on her aunt, she might be able to keep her alive and get her healed with Synol.

Meki blasted the Queen once again with a massive gust of icy wind. Two large ice sheets surged up from the floor, pushing both beasts out of the way.

Huge hunks of ice slammed into the wall where the Queen stood, pelting her body with an overwhelming barrage of magic. Over and over, Meki threw whatever hunks of ice she could summon at the Queen, pinning her to the wall and preventing her from moving.

The Queen blocked and dodged, but every barrage took its toll. With every attack, the Queen's magic grew weaker, while Meki's grew stronger.

The sheer volume of magic thrown between the two was beyond astonishing. Meki was determined to use up all of her and the Queen's magic in one massive blizzard.

The entire room was covered in a thick layer of ice, and an icy fog filled the air, making it difficult to breathe.

Ynya, pouring all of her heat into her Aunt, shivered in the cold. Her fingers and toes were blue, and the tingling sensation in her extremities had turned into a throbbing warmth.

Winds whipped in a cyclone of terror as the seemingly boundless well of magic drained into the room from both Meki and the Queen as they battled one another.

With each spell cast, the Queen grew weaker, but so did Meki.

Ynya poured more heat into her Aunt, laying across her to try to keep her mother's sister from dying after her heroic betrayal.

Finally, the winds stopped.

Chapter Thirty-Four

"Ynya!" Meki called. "I need the silver earring!"

Nora, barely alive at this point, opened her hand slowly, revealing both earrings. The pain from her injuries was palpable on her frigid face. "Give it to her. She is going to lock the Queen away from her magic, but she needs the earring to do so."

Ynya looked between the earrings, her Aunt's face, and Meki.

Meki held her hand out. "Just give it to me! I have nearly all of our power drained, so I need to stop my magic. I can't let her pull the rest from me!"

Ynya thought she understood, but was still confused how her eight-year-old sister had come up with such a plan.

Ynya remembered back to when she was eight, fighting the frost bear known as Yolphinir. She had been pretty clever back then, hadn't she? Meki was just finally able to show her own strength for once, rather than being known as the baby of the family.

Or worse yet, a slave to the Queen.

Ynya looked at the earrings in Nora's hand. She couldn't give Meki the bronze one. It couldn't be taken back out, but the silver one could always be removed later so Meki had her magic once again.

Ynya grabbed the silver earring from her Aunt's hand, and tossed it to Meki.

Meki grabbed the earring, opened it, and shoved it through her ear. She crumpled to the table, exhausted from the battle.

Ynya surveyed the room.

Everything and everyone was covered in a thick layer of ice and snow. The vast majority covered the wall, trapping the Frost Queen.

Both hounds were once again trapped in an icy cage, but they were busy burrowing themselves out.

Synol was covered in a thick layer of frost and ice.

Behind her, the Frost Queen struggled to pull in magic to lash out. If left alone, she would escape her icy prison in a matter of minutes and the fight would start all over again.

With the Queen incapacitated, Ynya's magic flooded her body with a vengeance. She had enough to thaw out her sisters, melt through the ice, and hopefully enough to keep the Queen frozen in time to escape.

"I can kill the Queen right now. I have the magic to stop time."

Nora shook her head. Her voice was weak and strained. "No, you can't. Her magic will protect her. The same magic that she used to poison Synol will never go away, and any attempt on her life will just end yours.

"See what it did to me? There is no tricking it, if you try to take her life, it will only end in your sacrifice. The only one who can kill her is a member of her family. You need to run, Ynya. Run with your sisters and get to safety."

"But–"

"No!" Nora bit back sharply. "You don't have any time left. You must thaw out the exit, and get your sisters out of here. You don't have time to do anything else. You have a narrow window, now act!"

Ynya nodded, hot tears streaming down her cheeks.

Ynya used her time magic to freeze the Queen in time, along with maintaining her sister Synol. The more she used her mother's magic, the more comfortable she was, able to target specific spots to freeze in time. She was improving, and she had enough power built up inside her that she should be able to easily fend off the army to help them escape.

"Take my dagger. You might need it."

Ynya wordlessly took her Aunt's dagger and its sheath, then grabbed the bronze earring from Nora's hand and laid a warm hand on her Aunt's face.

"I'm sorry it came to this. I'm sorry we didn't have enough time to spend together."

Nora smiled, a weak, strained action. "I love you, Ynya. I love all of you, and I'm proud to be your aunt. I'm sorry it took Synol nearly dying for me to realize how much I care for you."

The Skarmyord closed her eyes, reopening them with the void just like her sister had done a couple months prior. "I suppose it makes some sense to keep the magic of the Obliques living. Take my magic. It should help you survive."

Nora grabbed Ynya's face with her icy hands, and poured her magic into Ynya.

Beside Ynya's heart, next to the hardened time magic, and the hot fire magic, grew another magic, a sparking, jumpy source of power.

With a grunt, Nora Oblique died frozen to the ground.

Ynya wiped her eyes of tears and turned to warm up her sister.

She worked quickly and efficiently, warming up Synol's body, then making sure Meki was warm and awake. She helped melt the ice so that both beasts could break out of their cages, then melted a hole through the ice to allow them to escape the room

"I will take Meki. You and Synol will ride Pain," Finny told Ynya.

Ynya didn't argue. She and Meki hoisted Synol to Finny's back, then Meki climbed up on the other beast. And together, they all exited the dining room.

Chapter Thirty-Five

F inny crept down the hallways, growling and snapping at any maid or servant they found. Most of them hid in corners as they saw the beast coming at them.

Ynya followed behind, holding onto Synol's lifeless body.

Hang in there, big sis, we are going to get you out of here.

Whenever they came across a guard, Ynya froze them in time for long enough that they could slink past.

Handling the guards one at a time with her magic turned out to be the easiest method for leaving the castle.

No guards had to die, and they walked out with no casualties.

Except my Aunt sacrificed herself to help us escape. Never forget Nora.

Ynya fought back the tears that threatened to overwhelm her.

The entire time, Ynya held the Queen frozen, but as she got farther and farther away, the thread binding them grew more difficult to maintain.

Ynya was tired. Meki was barely conscious, and the beasts couldn't fight well enough with them on their backs.

They arrived on the ground floor of the castle.

Dozens of workers looked up, confusion on their faces as they tried to make sense of the two dark beasts and the girls riding them.

Ynya yelled to the group of tradesman. "The Queen is frozen for a short time, if you want to escape, now is your chance! Her heartbeat magic that forces you to work tirelessly and to her rhythm is gone, so run while you can!"

Some ran, but some still stood there, dumbfounded.

Finny took a step toward the exit, but Pain didn't move.

Finny turned around, growling.

Pain whimpered, but turned toward the staircase that led to the underground area.

"What is going on?" Ynya asked.

Finny growled. "The army is out front, and they are still loyal to the Queen. If we go out the front, you will need to stop time on all of them, or we will need to fight. He says he knows of another exit through the side that they used to bring him in weeks ago."

"Do you trust him?"

Finny looked over at Ynya, narrowing her eyes. "I do."

Ynya nodded. "Then I do, too. Pain, lead the way."

Pain led them down into the basement, stopping to sniff at the laboratory. He grunted and Finny translated. "He said there is a book down here with a lot of their experiments. He thinks we should take it. There is also food for the workers that you should grab to keep your energy up."

"What about you?"

Finny opened her mouth, showing off her teeth. "Pain and

I can hunt, but we won't be able to cook anything till we are far away, so grab what you can now."

Ynya did, finding a stockpile of hardened rolls and salted meat, along with a small keg of wine. She also found the book Pain had talked about, and stuffed that into a bag before remounting the beasts.

She also managed to find some rope and leather straps to bind Synol to Pain easier. They would need a better long-term solution, but for now this would have to do.

Ynya munched on one of the rolls and took a swig of the wine to help replenish her power. It wasn't much, but it would have to do. Given her depleted state, the wine went straight to her head and Ynya had to concentrate all the harder to keep all her spells up.

Pain then led them through to the back of the animal pens.

Far behind them, the shouts of the soldiers wafted over the sounds of the animals.

We're being followed! Regardless of the Queen's incapacitation, she still had her army.

They needed to hurry.

Pain came to a large iron door set in the back wall.

"This leads up to the surface and dumps out on the east side of the castle, about a mile away. They have to know we're going for this but they will have to fight the snow and we can run faster than them. If we hurry, we can make it there before they defend it."

They opened the door and entered. The tunnel was surprisingly large. A small wagon could easily fit through there, making it easy for them to bring in animals without having to take them through the main gate.

Before leaving, however, Ynya hopped off and melted parts of the door, fusing the corners to the frame and bending the door such that it couldn't move without an immense amount of effort.

"This should buy us some time."

Time.

It had all been down to time, hadn't it? From the moment her mother gifted her magic, it had always been about discovering and using the newfound ability.

Now that Ynya had it, she wondered how different her quest would have been if she had managed to figure it out sooner.

Ynya shook her head, clearing the haze in her mind. She needed to pay attention to what they did right now, in this moment.

The beasts were incredibly fast. Even with the small party on their backs, they ran up the slope with ease, bursting through the door up top and into the blinding snow.

Ynya hopped off and incapacitated the two guards who had been stationed at the entrance. She took all of their supplies and their swords. She also stripped them of their coats and bundled up her sisters so they wouldn't freeze.

The wind from the east bit into Ynya's skin, but she had poured so much magic into the thread of the Frost Queen that she couldn't keep herself warm any longer.

"Ynya, you should drop her. She won't be able to escape and track us down fast enough. We're free." Meki wrapped her arms around Ynya.

Ynya hugged back.

"I know."

Ynya took a few steps back, looking up at the sheer cliff face that had been her latest prison.

"There's no way we are going to make it past the army now, and we need to head west to get home."

Finny growled. "We will have to head south and go around them."

Ynya sighed. "She's going to come after us."

Meki squeezed harder. "Don't worry about it, my big sister will figure out something for us to do."

Ynya smiled down at Meki. "I'm glad you think that. We have a long road ahead of us still, but we're all together finally, and we will figure out a way to stay that way."

Ynya mounted Pain once again.

She looked back at the massive rock, hearing the shouts of the soldiers in the distance.

Ynya dropped her time magic on the Queen as Pain turned toward the west and bounded through the snow.

"Come after me, you bitch. I'll be ready for you."

Epilogue

Imryll Farora sat in her icy prison for a long time as she contemplated the events that had led to her defeat.

She wasn't mad that she had been betrayed by one of her own Skarmyord. Humans were emotional and reactionary creatures by nature.

She wasn't upset that Ynya's magic had been so close to her grasp, but now bounded off into the east. Ynya couldn't escape the Feond, so she wasn't going anywhere.

She wasn't bothered by the fact that four human girls had managed to thwart her efforts.

She was irritated with herself. She had let them get the best of her, and she knew it. She had spent far too long believing she was untouchable.

She learned a valuable lesson.

She would not make that mistake again.

She had been bested by four untrained, and barely bloomed girls. The irony was heavy in her mind. She'd been so young and untrained herself back when she discovered her father's true plans for the elves.

She had been very similar to Ynya in that matter. She was young and unafraid, willing to take un-calculated risks that sometimes worked out for the worst.

Young people could be so surprising.

Humans, for that matter, could as well.

Still, there were natural orders to things, rules that needed to be enforced.

"My lady." Khatar stood at the entrance to the dining room.

She growled. She was enjoying the silence. For once the constant howl of the wind hadn't penetrated into her cocoon of ice. For once she relished in the sounds of silence.

Perhaps she would construct one of these chambers for meditation later. Right now, it was time to wrest control back from her disheveled minions.

Imryll shattered the ice holding her against the wall.

She stood, dusting the small ice chips off her dress.

"Khatar, send word to the commanders of the army. I need them to pull their troops back so we can plan properly. I expect all five of them to be back here shortly."

Khatar hesitated, looking like he wanted to second guess her instructions. Normally, she would have punished such a delay in her commands, but right now she had other things on her mind.

Seeming satisfied, Khatar nodded his head and replied. "As you wish, Your Majesty."

"Oh, and Khatar, I want all their lieutenants to come as well."

"Of course."

Imryll walked over to the stiff, lifeless body of her head captain. She stared down at the woman for a while, taking in every line of her face. Nora had been a beautiful woman, a troublemaker her entire life, always doing things of her own accord, regardless of the consequences.

But she had been effective. Her betrayal had been inevitable, but her role in the larger plan had been fulfilled.

Talia's magic had been exposed.

Imryll bent down to stroke Nora's frozen face. "I knew you hid Talia's magic from me all these years, Nora. I knew, and I never pressed you on it. I hope you know that I could have tortured it out of you at any point, but I trusted that you were holding back on me this whole time, and I was right."

Imryll stood. "And now I have Talia and your magic closer than ever to me. Ynya doesn't even know what seed of magic she carries within her, nor do the other two, but I will get it back, and it will be the key to my eventual reign."

Imryll used her magic to stomp her boot into Nora Oblique's chest, shattering the frozen body into thousands of fleshy red chunks.

"At least your sacrifice wasn't in vain. I see my mistakes now and will correct them."

She stood there for what seemed forever, mulling over the possibilities. She took time to explore how each betrayal came about, and formed plans to prevent those in the future.

"My Lady. They await in your study."

Imryll looked up.

"Ahh yes, thank you, Khatar."

She contemplated her new reality for a bit longer before heading up. She needed to make sure her message was conveyed in just the right manner.

Her top commanders stood at attention in the center of her study. Their immediate subordinates directly behind them.

"Captain Nora's death was unfortunate, but necessary. I

see that now. I see that I hadn't been paying close enough attention to the most trusted among me."

To her side, one of the captains began to choke as ice filled his lungs.

Beside him, the next one choked.

In a matter of seconds, five commanders, each in charge of their own contingents of soldiers stood in place, their bodies having been frozen from the inside out.

She eyed each of her new subordinates. "As you see, I will stop at nothing to achieve my goals, so I want you to take this little demonstration back to your troops with a message. We will succeed, or I will personally go down the rank of every one of your troops and freeze their lungs until they die."

She snapped her fingers and the five commanders shattered. Each of their frozen heads landed in the arms of their successor.

"Now go, my new commanders."

Khatar stood for a long time while she watched the new leaders of the army sprint out of the castle and into their troops.

She looked to her sides, taking in the figures on spikes. How long had it been since she had put them up there? She thought that by leaving them up as a testament to their failures, she would have instilled the proper fear in her soldiers, but clearly humans forgot too easily. They needed to be reminded sometimes of their own fallibility.

"Khatar, I think it's time we brought down my old lieutenants, don't you think? It's time for some new leadership in my ranks."

THE END

I HOPE YOU ENJOYED THIS BOOK! IF YOU DID, PLEASE leave a review on Amazon or Goodreads. Reviews help others find my books, which means I can continue to write more like this!

Thank you so much for reading, and I hope you check out the next episode in The Frost Fervor Concordance!

- Tom Hansen

December 2018

Author's Notes

December 2018

This book was a struggle.

I had plans on wrapping up something major with this book, but, as many other authors like to say, the characters have a mind of their own.

The biggest issue was the ending. I envisioned a grand climax, but by the time the girls managed to escape the icy clutches of the Frost Queen, I had ran out of room to properly build up for the big reveal.

That meant I either needed to add significantly to the length of this book, or I needed to end the story and address it in another book.

I chose the second option.

It wasn't easy to decide either. I had to give the entire first draft to my wife, along with my weak attempt at wrapping up this book (I tried to write the whole ending) to get her opinion.

She suggested I spend more time fleshing out the next plot point in the series.

And thus, the book was split, and you will see what I had planned in the next book.

It wasn't my original plan, but the story will be better for it.

If you loved this book, please leave a review on Amazon. Reviews help others find my books, which means I can continue to write more like this!

I realize Amazon does't make it easy to leave a review because you can't just hit stars and move on, but even a simple review like "You go, Finny!" goes a long way to letting others know that this series is worth checking out.

Sharing the book with others on social media helps get the word out. So hop on the Twitters and the Instagrams. Shout from the top of the Facebooks and the Reddits that you love my story!

While you're there, come say hi! I love to hear how my stories have entertained or touched you.

Finally, I have so many other stories to tell in this universe, and I've already written one that I want to share with you. Consider signing up to my newsletter so you can be notified of future releases!

Thank you so much for reading, and I'll see you next time!

- Tom Hansen

December 2018

Excerpt from Sparking Vengeance

BOOK FOUR OF THE FROST FERVOR
CONCORDANCE

Unedited Draft Chapter

Ynya Oblique coughed for the third time since she had woken up. Minute blood droplets splattered the frozen ground with each excruciating hack of her lungs.

Meki frowned. "Are you okay?"

Ynya sat back down, her wracking chest finally subsiding. "I'll be fine, don't worry about me."

Meki handed her a warm mug of water, then pursed her lips, mirroring a similar action from Synol.

Ynya chanced a look at their slumbering sister, frozen in time by her own magic. The black lines of the Frost Queen's poison ran up Synol's neck, stopping just at her hairline. Each one hungered to continue north, to consume and eradicate Synol from the world.

Ynya would not allow it.

But something was wrong with Ynya, and it didn't seem physical. Ever since they had made it away from the Frost Queen's castle, something had been off.

Three days later, they were out of food, out of energy, and Ynya had been spitting up blood for most of a day.

Meki finally noticed this morning when she woke up and found frozen blood on Ynya's cheek.

"We need to find someone to take care of you."

Ynya glanced over to Finny, who had taken her human form once again. "I smell a small settlement not far from here, about nine miles to the west."

Behind Finny, Pain, her twisted wolf-like companion whined. Finny turned and laid a hand on his neck. He quieted and nuzzled his head into her stomach.

Ynya had to admit, despite their horrifying mottled skin and spines instead of fur, they both had a mortifying charm about them. Their bestial forms were conjured in the worst circumstances imaginable, and yet through their torture, had found each other.

Ynya shook her head at the ida. "We can't risk it, it's right along the main road leading away from Fangorn Castle, the Queen will know where we are."

Meki folded her arms. "She already knows where we are. Just because we're further away from her doesn't mean the bond disappeared. If can feel where she is, then she can do the same."

Finny nodded. "I, too, in beast form, can feel her. She knows where we are at any moment. Pain doesn't have that problem, possibly an oversight when they made him, but they corrected it with me."

Ynya didn't like where any of this conversation was headed, and as the oldest one here, she had a responsibility to get them somewhere safe. "We need to keep moving, it's our only chance to stay ahead of her and eventually find out way back home."

Ynya stood, planning on grabbing her small pack and continuing the slog through the snow, but her head swam and her exhausted legs gave out.

"Ynya!"

Meki yelling her name was the last thing she remembered before the world blacked out.

Ynya woke.

Her normal dreams of her mother hadn't come this time. In fact, the only dream she had was of four figures trudging through the snow in an endless quest.

She looked around, finding herself in a small hut. Thatched roof supported by rough timbers above her told her the girls must have brought her to the near village, despite her reticence.

Despite the small cottage, it was light enough in here that she could see fairly clearly. A handful of pots hung from the rafters along with an assortment of kitchen utensils.

She tried to sit up, but a hand on her chest held her down.

"Oh no, miss. You're not supposed to move." It was a male voice, deep and slow.

A male voice attached to a hairy male arm that touched her chest!

Ynya recoiled as her mind raced.

Where was she? Was she dreaming? Had her sisters abandoned her? What was going on?

Two strong, warm hands grabbed her shoulders. "Miss, please. My sister will be back soon. I'm supposed to watch you and keep you here."

"Where are my sisters? Who are you? Please take your hands off me!"

Ynya's voice was shrill and high-pitched, and the sudden

rush of shock quickened her heart and lungs enough to send her into a coughing fit.

She bent over, trying to cough off the side of the small bed. The dirt floor was lined with straw, and she coughed up more blood onto it. After a few wracks, her lungs calmed down and she sat back up, wiping blood off her mouth.

The man handed her a handkerchief. "For the blood. Sister told me to give to you if you coughed."

Sign up for my newsletter to be notified when Sparking Vengeance releases!

About Tom Hansen

THE CREATIVE CURMUDGEON

Fantastic worlds. Get-Off-My-Lawn attitude.

Tom Hansen is the writer and lover of all things fantasy. While he can't seem to stick to a specific genre, you can rest assured that anything he writes will have that aspect of whimsy and world building that defines the fantasy genre.

His first series is the *End Gate Chronicles* is a modern-day urban fantasy following an older widow, who discovers her own magic late in life.

His second series, *Enter the louVRe*, is set inside a video game, where an evil AI has trapped players and stolen their memories. Now, our hero, a minotaur, must save the world from destruction if he is to have any hope of unraveling the AI's plans and escape the game unscathed.

His third series, *The Frost Fervor Concordance*, is set in a fantastical frozen wasteland, where a young fisher comes home to find her village burned and her parents killed. The fire-headed mage must track down her kidnapped sisters and battle the tyrannical Frost Queen in order to keep her sisters safe.

Tom lives in Arizona with his dear wife, four children, and two cats.

To follow Tom, check out his website or any of the link below:
www.scarhoof.com

- facebook.com/scarhoof
- twitter.com/scarhoof
- amazon.com/author/tomhansen
- bookbub.com/authors/tom-hansen-7a3f964c-dbe3-4b40-a702-f7c60c91c3b3
- goodreads.com/scarhoof
- youtube.com/scarhoofplays
- instagram.com/Scarhoof

Also by Tom Hansen

WWW.SCARHOOF.COM/ALSOBYTOMHANSEN

Adventure Fantasy

THE FROST FERVOR CONCORDANCE:

Inciting Vengeance (Prequel Novella)

Igniting Vengeance (#1)

Flaming Vengeance (#2)

Blazing Vengeance (#3)

Sparking Vengeance (Coming Mid 2019)

Flaring Vengeance (Coming Late 2019)

Burning Vengeance (Coming Late 2019)

BUNDLES:

The Frost Fervor Concordance Trilogy (Books 1-3 + bonus Novella!)

SHORT FICTION:

Ynya vs the Frost Bear (Prequel Short)

LitRPG/GameLit

ENTER THE louVRe SERIES:

Mightier Still (Prequel Novella)

Eloria's Beginning (#1)

Eloria's Calling (Coming Early 2020)

Urban Fantasy

END GATE SERIES:

A Moonlit Task

Mayhem in the Moonlight (Coming Mid 2019)

Secrets of the Shadowed Moon (Coming Mid 2019)

THE KORRIGAN CHRONICLES:

The Sacking of Gildebrand Manor

That Dammed Berehynia

Moloch's Twisted Menagerie

Freya's Wild Hunt

The Roswell Incident

Short Fiction/Anthologies

Into the Void: A Steampunk Short Story

Glimpses: an Anthology of 16 Short Fantasy Stories

Futurism & Fantasia: Volume 1: First Chapters

Newsletter Exclusives

Miss-Miss's Near Miss (Adventure Fantasy)

Splashes of Wine (Urban Fantasy)

The Curious Case of Brendalynn Bobbins (LitRPG)